D1744582

EVERYDAY FOLKS

A SHORT STORY COLLECTION

Volume 2

BILLY P. JONES

EVERYDAY FOLKS, VOLUME 2
A SHORT STORY COLLECTION

Copyright © 2019 Billy P. Jones.

All rights reserved. No part of this book may be used or reproduced by any means, graphic, electronic, or mechanical, including photocopying, recording, taping or by any information storage retrieval system without the written permission of the author except in the case of brief quotations embodied in critical articles and reviews.

This is a work of fiction. All of the characters, names, incidents, organizations, and dialogue in this novel are either the products of the author's imagination or are used fictitiously.

iUniverse books may be ordered through booksellers or by contacting:

iUniverse
1663 Liberty Drive
Bloomington, IN 47403
www.iuniverse.com
1-800-Authors (1-800-288-4677)

Because of the dynamic nature of the Internet, any web addresses or links contained in this book may have changed since publication and may no longer be valid. The views expressed in this work are solely those of the author and do not necessarily reflect the views of the publisher, and the publisher hereby disclaims any responsibility for them.

Any people depicted in stock imagery provided by Getty Images are models, and such images are being used for illustrative purposes only. Certain stock imagery © Getty Images.

ISBN: 978-1-5320-8274-0 (sc)
ISBN: 978-1-5320-8275-7 (hc)
ISBN: 978-1-5320-8296-2 (e)

Library of Congress Control Number: 2019915263

Print information available on the last page.

iUniverse rev. date: 10/22/2019

To Fabio, Kipri, Betty A., Mima, Pop, family, friends…
and everyone who has inspired this book.
It's only fiction (smile).

Contents

Preface

"This book will never get published," I would tell myself. For 15 years, *Everyday Folks* remained in limbo.

Writing and work are two words that don't mix well. I made the choice to ride the corporate ladder, casting aside creative writing and independent thinking at times.

I teach English Composition, Literature and Creative Writing courses at a community college. Daily, I encourage my students to "make time for writing." On many occasions I didn't practice what I was preaching. Even though the struggle continued, the writing never stopped.

In one of my 2017 podcasts, a fan asked me, "What happens when you just can't write anymore?"

My answer was simple. *Writing never stops.* Yet the writing did stop… at least for me.

I was challenged to produce consistently because I was mentally exhausted from professional and personal life. I created a "love-hate" relationship with writing. In times when writing should have been my refuge, I turned my back on it because I saw it as a *task* versus the *enjoyment* it should always be. I told myself that if I were to rediscover my mental peace and reestablish a zest for life, I needed to change my attitude immediately toward the writing process. Writing is good therapy. It costs nothing yet offers everything... a perfect over-the-counter prescription.

As I met people, took trips, and visited places, I was so impacted by these experiences that I was compelled to write again. Every story is based on an experience shared to me by someone I know or have met over the past 14 years. All stories are purposely set in a fictional setting.

My biggest fan of my work is my book club. I have been an active member of a book club for nearly a decade now. Together, we have read more than 70 books of many talented authors. Each writer provided me new hope and meaning for my own writing. From the romantic streets of Barcelona, Spain, in *Shadow of the Wind* by Carlos Ruiz Zafon to the humor and southern charm of *Georgia Bottoms* by Mark Childress, not only the storylines, but also the language the writers crafted moved me. I was transported to another time and place on many nights. This literary excursion was the very medicine I needed to redefine my own existence in an evolving, creative world.

My family and dear friends know that in my private time, I'm a very simple person. Yet my mind is constantly moving and thinking about creative possibilities: What happens when we die? Why do people choose to do good things versus bad things? Are people more disinterested in reading today? How does love manifest in times of suffrage? From these simple, (sometimes) mundane questions, I have been able to create ideas based on true stories.

Most of the stories aren't about me. I find my life so predictable and less appealing. Honestly, I'm really not that interested in writing about what I already know. Instead I'm more interested in what others have to say. I love *people*. Every person has a story and many of those stories go untold. *EF* is a safe place for everyday people to escape their own realities and perhaps find understanding in their lives through reading about the lives of others, no matter how similar or distant those experiences may be.

I thank you, loyal reader, for your commitment. *EF* is back and here to stay.

Beware of the Gremlin

MANY PEOPLE LOVE "Hump Day Wednesdays" but I detested them all. They were the bearers of long, arduous cabinet meetings. The weekly entrapment was grueling. The night before, each of us cabinet members would prep our agenda items and strategically plan our positions around the "war table."

After my first meeting with my new boss and campus cabinet, I had an epiphany: Never trust anyone. The landscape looked that different.

Wednesday campus cabinet meetings weren't always so bad until HE arrived. He relished in sudden changes, resulting in a shift in campus leadership. Some saw *the storm* coming; they exited via resignation or retirement.

I heard the rumors about his arrival, and worse, his leadership style. My colleague told me a story of how he would embarrass workers if a cellphone sounded during one of his meetings. She also remembered people crying behind closed doors in their offices or other obscure spaces. I knew my place. If I breathed too hard, I would have been served a pink slip on firing week in May.

And speaking of May...

He contributed to the start of a blackout week preceding Memorial Day. For about a decade, it was well known that executive firings would take place on this week. I watched as talented professionals held on to the hopes of surviving another grueling season of "I made it pass hell week" frenzy.

His name was Ramon Rodriguez. No one could imagine that something so short and small could harbor such horrible, evil forces. Standing five-feet, six-inches, he wasn't a physical threat. He reminded me of the kid who was bullied in my seventh-grade physical education class... who eventually grew up and became super cool. Ramon liked to dress in dark suits and expected his executive committee to do so too. He had the Napoleon Complex, boasting his authority incessantly during special events and formal occasions. He ruled through fear—all under the guise of "professional excellence."

I watched him turn allies into bitter enemies. When he was in a good mood, meetings ran smoothly. But when had his fits of rage, all hell broke loose. That small frame would transform into something so grotesque, so vile, and so inhumane...

A Gremlin. The evil belonged to a unique species after all.

Gremlins were small creatures in the hit 80s movie, *The Gremlins*. The protagonist, Billy, purchased one and took it home. In order to take care of it, he was instructed to do three things.

Rule Number One: Never expose it to sunlight. Movie spoiler, when Gremlins were exposed, they became ugly creatures capable of doing mischievous things.

Rule Number Two: Never feed them after midnight. Gremlins had insatiable appetites. Feeding them after midnight only added to the adverse effect.

*And Rule Number Three: Never get them wet…*For they would multiply. Having one Gremlin in the world was enough. I couldn't bare the thought of them populating.

I warned Victoria to be careful around the Gremlin. As the Student Dean, she performed her duties well for nearly five years. Prior to her appointment, she served as the department chairperson of one of the largest disciplines in the college. Her credentials matched her potential too, for she possessed a Ph.D. and a J.D. from two of the most prestigious institutions in the world. Her intellect matched her personality. People loved her and were rarely fired under her watch. They left for two reasons: either they went on to better endeavors or they retired. I marveled how her strength and integrity. She was my Latina sister born and raised in the Dominican Republic.

As her "work husband," I knew she had her flaws. She was "flighty" in her approaches at times. And it didn't help that she was blond. Because her native language was Spanish, Victoria sometimes had to think more critically about her delivery in meetings or other communications. I defended her when others gossiped, questioning her leadership abilities. I knew that she was aware of what was occurring, and that bothered me. The woman didn't deserve that type of treatment, no matter how obscure or covert it was.

Wednesday, September 4, 2014, arrived. I grew miserable as I trekked the corridor to Ramon's conference room in the Campus President's suite. My feet felt like they were made of lead. As I stood at the suite's door, I took a deep breath and entered.

Victoria arrived just seconds before me. She and I were usually the first ones at the meeting. I noticed the look on her face; something disturbed her. Her assistant warned her about a potential "tear down" at our meeting related to campus enrollment. Victoria came prepared with a thick, three-ringed binder. Her binder was filled with the latest enrollment data: enrollment data by discipline, by popular courses, by projection, and by previous three-years' standings. To the average person, the numbers and graphics were a foreign language or complex math equation. To Victoria, these data were weaponry for the "battlefield," our meeting. I smiled at her. I knew our friendship would be challenged soon enough.

"How do I look?" I asked Victoria, turning around and allowing her to give me the "once over" look.

"You look handsome, Roger," she approved. We took our seats, sitting across from one another.

I wore more dapper suits than the Gremlin, and he despised this at times. Those who disliked Roman would compliment my dress style in front of him. I wore a navy blue suit and a Kelly green tie. My classic Swatch watch was a mixture of both colors.

I preferred sitting to the left of the Gremlin to peek at personal notes and scribbles. The Gremlin would occasionally remind me to stay in my lane. I did the opposite, choosing to save another wounded comrade on the battlefield.

We peered over our binders while waiting for others to arrive.

"Did you bring the *latest* enrollment numbers?" I asked with concern.

"Yes, I always do," she replied.

"Good. You know he'll be expecting them, especially since this is the third week of the term," I said.

"Yes, and so far, we're up 5%. Other campuses are down," Victoria said reviewing the figures. Thank goodness. The morning was off to a good start.

Danielle, the Honors Dean, arrived next. She was the newest addition to the cabinet. Originally from New York, she traded her snow boots for sandals and sunshine dollars. At her previous institution, she worked as an Assistant Dean and former director. She came highly recommended to the college. Armed with a J.D. of her own, she was well versed in legal affairs. The Gremlin liked her very much.

"Good morning," Danielle chimed.

"Good morning," Victoria and I replied in unison. Danielle walked over to the refreshment table and poured herself a cup of coffee. The smell of Starbucks classic filled the air. Victoria got up to grab a cup as well.

The door opened again, and James entered. James was the Vice Provost of the Arts School. A classically trained violinist, James had an ear for great talent and an even better one for detecting the evil forces of the Gremlin. Raised in Arkansas, he had adapted to South Florida life well over the span of 15 years. It was rumored that he would be the next Campus President when the Gremlin retired. Overall, he was well liked and respectful... and respected. I teased him periodically about his Grammy award, which he displayed proudly in his office.

"Hi," James greeted.

"Good morning, James," I responded.

"Hi," chimed the two women in unison.

The conversations continued. James talked about his weekend trip while I applauded Danielle's impressive enrollment figures. Victoria smiled and looked on. The rest of us were exchanging all sorts of small talk; however, it was hard for Victoria to join (and sometimes keep up) with the conversations.

Ten minutes later, it appeared. The Gremlin entered with his executive assistant, Mary, a few steps behind him. She carried his cobalt-colored coffee cup. He wore the usual navy blue suit with a patriotic red and white tie. He looked like a politician who was campaigning for public office. We stopped chatting. The Gremlin took his spot at the head of the table, which was located near the door.

"Good morning," he boomed.

"Good morning," everyone chimed.

"It's a beautiful morning in Miami... is that a yes or a yes?" He asked trying to be funny.

Everyone "fake" chuckled, but me.

"Yes, it is," I said.

"Great. You have the agenda. Mary has extra copies in case you need one," he said. He opened his leather portfolio and pulled out his pen. He was left-handed.

"You also had a chance to review the minutes sent out previously. Are there any changes?" He asked. We shook our heads or remained silent. "Seeing there are no changes, is there a motion to approve the minutes?"

"So moved," I replied.

"Seconded," James followed.

"Okay, all in favor?" He asked.

"Aye," all responded.

"All opposed?" Silence followed. "The minutes are approved."

The Gremlin sifted through his records.

"How is enrollment?" He inquired, looking at Victoria.

"Very good," I began. "We are up 5%..."

"Wait, I prefer to hear it from the Student Dean," the Gremlin interrupted.

I remained quiet. I gave Victoria an earnest look. I prayed her nerves wouldn't get the better of her.

"Well...enrollment is good. We are up 5%," Victoria said.

"Compared to other campuses?" he asked.

"We are the only campus on the positive side," she said.

"Very good..." He said. He looked across the table at James. James froze. The Gremlin's Emerald green eyes were menacing. When he stared at someone, usually he was foreshadowing something to happen. I had seen that stare a hundred times.

"I have a question," the Gremlin began.

He returned his gaze to Victoria, and he continued, "How are we doing on the calls for financial aid students? You know, the report that shows the students who have completed and were approved for aid but never registered? The college-wide list indicates more than 5,000 students. What's our plan?"

"Well, uh, we have a very good plan..." Victoria stuttered.

"That's not what I asked. What is it? Get to the point," he retorted.

I slowly watched as Victoria's confidence slipped into oblivion. Ramon knew something, and worse, he knew he could intimidate her.

"My staff has made the calls," she continued.

"Who made the calls?" Ramon asked.

"My directors, Janis and Delores," she replied.

"And when did they make the calls?" he asked.

"Last week," Victoria responded. She glanced at me. There was nothing I could do. His badgering was so relentless.

"And out of the number of calls that were made, how many callbacks did we get?" he inquired.

"About 100 each director," she said.

"Hmm," he sounded. He stared in the distance at the wall behind Danielle's head. She sat directly across from him at the conference table. I could cut the silence with a knife. None of us moved or fumbled through papers. All eyes were on the Gremlin.

"Call your directors and have them here in five minutes. We'll take a short break. When I get back, we'll continue," the Gremlin said and exited the room. His assistant followed him.

Victoria unlocked her cellphone and began making the calls. Janis and Delores were immediately available and in route to the conference room. Victoria hung up the phone and looked at me.

"He's fishing for something, Victoria," I warned.

"I know," she said. She looked almost defeated.

"Is there anything we can do to help you?" Danielle asked.

"No, but thank you," Victoria responded.

Minutes later, Janis and Delores entered the room. Each woman carried her portfolio, which contained essential documents. They sat opposite sides of Victoria.

The Gremlin returned shortly after. Maria followed.

"Good morning, ladies," he started in a serious tone. "I need you to clarify a few things."

"Yes," they nodded. They were so nervous.

"And you've come prepared?" he asked.

"Yes," they chimed in unison.

"Tell me, who made the calls last week for your respective departments?"

"My assistant made my calls," Janis started.

"And what is her name?"

"Nicole."

"And how many calls did she make?"

"A little over a hundred."

"And out of those calls, how many callbacks did she receive?"

"25," Janis replied.

"Okay," he turned to address Delores. "And how many calls were made last week in your area?"

"Over a hundred," Delores responded.

"And out of the hundred calls, how many callbacks did you receive?" he inquired.

"1," Delores said, holding up her left-pointing finger.

"Hmm, only 1 call out of 100? And who made these calls?"

"Julio, my student assistant," Delores answered.

"I see…" The Gremlin stared back at the blank space behind Danielle's head. An eerie ten seconds passed in absolute silence. He turned to address Victoria.

"So as Student Dean, you're telling me that your area has been able to accomplish 200 calls? How many names are on our campus list?" he asked.

"About 700," Victoria said. She shifted in her seat.

"Hmm…" he paused. "Let's get Julio and Nicole on the phone. When I come back, please have each of them on the line." He left the room.

Victoria pulled out her phone once more to speak to her assistant. She instructed her to locate Julio and Nicole immediately. Meanwhile, Delores and Janis texted them. Within five minutes, Julio and Nicole were on hold on the conference phone line. I watched fear envelop those poor colleagues. We were all defenseless against the Gremlin.

And when it returned, he had a serious look. His chipper mood had disappeared.

Maria pressed the buttons on the conference phone. Nicole was on standby on line one.

"Hello, Nicole. This is the Campus President and you're on the phone with the executive cabinet of the campus. I have a question for you," the Gremlin said in a forceful tone.

"Good morning, sir," Nicole greeted the group, slightly nervous.

"We are determining how many calls were made during the past week regarding the financial aid student list. It's my understanding that you've made some calls on behalf of your supervisor?"

"Yes, I have," she answered.

"And how many calls did you make?"

"About 100 calls."

"And out of the 100 calls, how many callbacks did you receive?" he asked.

"26," Nicole said.

"Excellent! Thank you. And how are you handling the remaining names on the list? It is my understanding that there are 700 students who need to be called."

"We have divided the workload. The calls will be completed over the next two days," Nicole assured.

"Thank you. And thank you for your time." Nicole hung up the phone.

I was so proud of Victoria in that moment. Victoria winked at me. Her confidence was slowly returning.

"Next caller," Ramon nudged.

Moments later, Julio, who was holding on line two, spoke.

"Hello?" Julio started.

"Julio, this is the Campus President and you are with the executive cabinet of the campus. We have a question for you…" the Gremlin repeated.

"Yes, how can I help you?" Julio asked.

He didn't sound too nervous. I looked at Delores and noticed her sad, pleading eyes. Something was wrong.

"It is my understanding that you've made a few calls on behalf of your supervisor regarding the college-wide financial aid list," Ramon continued.

"I did, sir, yes," Julio said.

"And how many calls did you make?" He asked.

"Wait…Calls? I didn't make any calls. The last calls I made were back in April," Julio confessed.

I looked down. I felt a sharp pain in my stomach. My intuition was right.

"Oh," the Gremlin responded in surprise, staring coldly at Delores and Victoria over the rim of his glasses and continued, "Your supervisors seem to disagree."

"No, sir, I'm sure," Julio said undeniably.

"Thank you, sir," the Gremlin pressed the button on the conference phone's console. The call ended.

We all experienced the most intense silence ever. I looked down at my paperwork. I grabbed my pen and began tapping it on the table; I knew what would happen next...

"Pathetic!" The Gremlin exclaimed. My eyes widened. I stared at my friend. He looked at Victoria and continued, "It's my expectation that as Student Dean you handle what is required of you. Pathetic!"

Janis and Delores were scared. They heard the stories but had not witnessed the evil firsthand. Today was an unfortunate day.

"You may leave, ladies," he said.

Janis and Delores exited. For the next hour, we all watched Roman roast Victoria. The future looked grim for her. I knew my dear colleagues were marked for potential termination.

Seven months later, the week before Memorial Day finally arrived. Weeks before, I joked with my office staff about my potential firing. I even went the extra mile of hoarding empty, large boxes. It was my way of coping with the inevitable power of the Gremlin.

That Wednesday afternoon, after another arduous cabinet meeting, I received a call Maria, Ramon's assistant. She called me to an emergency meeting at 4 p.m. in his office. The day had arrived. I was clueless as to why I was receiving a contractual non-renewal.

I grabbed my pen, paper, and keys. As I walked to the presidential suite, a million thoughts entered my mind. I couldn't think of a reason why he'd let me go, but then again, it didn't even matter.

When I arrived to the suite, I saw James. We both looked puzzled, not sure why the other was present. Wait, I thought. That bastard! James had to be the designated witness for my termination. He arrived empty-handed.

The Gremlin received an unexpected call from his supervisor, the College President, delaying our meeting. Mary offered us beverages that they both declined. I couldn't drink an ounce of liquid. James started at the art painting hanging on the while across from where he was sitting. We couldn't speak. The fear of unemployment consumed me.

"He's ready for you, you may enter," Mary said.

She escorted us to the Gremlin's lair.

He sat behind his desk, which was strewn with papers. Paper served as a tablecloth. Ramon appeared even smaller among the mess in his office.

"Thank you for coming on such short notice," he said.

"Okay," I stated, trying to sound positive.

"I need you to do something for me."

James and I stared at him. I was about to be fired.

"I need you… to execute the terminations for the campus," he said, smiling. His emerald green eyes peered over the rim of his glasses. "Have you done this before?"

"No," I responded. James shook his head.

"Good. I will be taking tomorrow off. Randie, the HR Provost, will be calling you within the hour. She will prep you on the procedure and provide you an electronic script to read during the termination."

Then the Gremlin slid two sheets of paper to us. I took my sheet and began reading. It contained a list of seven names, and I knew every single one.

The names were of my colleagues who suffered that fateful day on Wednesday, September 4th. My dead friend, Victoria, was at the top of the list. The second and third names were Janis and Delores'. I felt a knot in my throat.

"And when you send your Outlook notices, send them right before you leave campus tonight. As soon as you do, leave. Any questions?"

"No," we uttered.

"Thank you. Have a great evening," he said.

James and I walked out together and we still didn't speak. I know he was hurting. But hurting people was part of our jobs.

The next afternoon, I had terminated everyone assigned to me. There were no dear farewells or departing words. Instead the campus was engulfed with fear. I couldn't eat lunch. By the end of the day, I felt like a zombie, numb to pain yet yearning for the taste of answers.

I finally told my office staff. They felt my pain; they didn't say a word, but their eyes spoke their feelings. They told me how Victoria's staff members tried emailing her or how colleagues tried calling Janis and Delores, but there were no replies. Everyone knew what time it was.

I was pissed as hell at the Gremlin. Someone should have read the warning label.

Rule Number one, broken: someone exposed the Gremlin to sunlight, causing it to fill with rage. Rule Number two, tarnished: someone fed it power and authority. The Gremlin used them for his personal gain. And the most important rule of all, Number Three, was disregarded: Never get it wet. As soon as the firings were completed, the Gremlin multiplied, hastily appointing his own kind to fill the leadership vacancies.

And Ramon went on to rule for another two years before his last-minute retirement announcement. By then, the damage was irreparable that he had caused. Fed up, I later resigned and moved to another college. James moved away with his significant other to explore international territories. Danielle was appointed interim Campus President at one of the college's smaller campuses.

I stayed in touch with them all, especially Victoria. After her termination, she returned to the Dominican Republic and was appointed Vice Chancellor of the college district.

We couldn't stop or kill the Gremlin, but we didn't let him win.

Miccosukee

"SOMETIMES MONEY is spent as fast as it's made. Life is about taking chances," Brenda thought.

She and her daughter, Emilee, ventured to the Miccosukee Resort & Gaming, Brenda's favorite hangout spot. Built near the Florida Everglades, the resort offered slot machines, free birthday meals, and international performances. Brenda and Emilee never stayed over night. They wanted to play a few slot machines and Black Jack while their men stayed home with the kids.

Brenda, a retired law enforcement officer, was stout and pretty. She defied aging, making it difficult for others to guess her age. Brenda was a good mother; she and Emilee were best friends. Emilee, a young mother of a two-year-old son, was vibrant and fun. She inherited her mother's beauty, wits, and attitude. With these two together, there was nothing they couldn't do. They were ready for a great Saturday afternoon.

Brenda drove to the resort. Heading south on Krome Avenue. The unique stretch of road ran from Florida City to South Broward. Truckers and tourists frequented it. Historically, Krome was known for its fatal accidents and nightly drag racing. Emilee wasn't a fan of the road. For the most part, she remained quiet as her mother, Brenda, drove the way.

"I'm so glad to get out that house," Brenda began.

"Me, too, Ma," Emilee added. "Love my son, but I need this moment."

"Well, Miccosukee, here we come!" Brenda exclaimed.

"Ma, make sure you don't overdue it this time," Emilee recommended.

"Yeah, yeah, I know my limits."

"But you said that last time, and you lost $200 in an hour. Be careful, Ma," Emilee said.

"Alright."

Brenda turned left onto 8th Street. Miccosukee Resort was just ahead to the right. Turning into the parking lot, she noticed several RV's and buses. Tourists, she thought. The resort would be packed with money spenders today.

After paying valet, Brenda and Emilee walked into the lobby. Cold air and cigarette smoke filled the air. Signage was everywhere. One particular sign read, "Win A 2015 Lexus" with an arrow pointing to the left. Brenda looked and spotted it, a blue Lexus four-door sedan sitting on a display platform. They looked at each other and smiled. The winning possibilities were endless.

They approached the card machines to exchange cash for a game card.

"Just put $75 this time, Ma," Emilee suggested.

"I'll put $100, just in case," Brenda replied.

"In case of what?" Emilee asked.

"I play to win, listen. Relax. I got this."

"Okay," Emilee said.

The ladies started with the slot machines, Brenda's favorite. For some reason, her luck was always pretty good with them. One time, she won $200, and she gave half of it to Emilee. Another time, she won $350, which she kept for herself. When she's feeling lucky, Brenda's right palm would itch. Today, however, her left palm itched. Her good luck muse was confusing her.

Joker's Wild was the name of slot machines. Each woman took her seat at the slots, right next to each other. Brenda took the play card and entered it into the payment slot then passed it over to Emilee, who did the same. Moments later, sounds of dings and spins filled the air. Brenda rolled two cherries and a dollar sign. The digital screen read $5. She pulled the lever again. This time, three cherries appeared and the machine went haywire. Her total spiked to $75. In a few minutes, Brenda managed to win $150.

Emilee, however, was not as lucky. After five tries, she won a mere $20. She glanced over at her mother's digital screen, which now read $250. Emilee's lack of luck increased her disinterest. She got up from the machine.

"I need a drink. Want something?" Emilee asked.

"I'm good, boo," Brenda responded.

Emilee left for the concession area.

Standing in line, she scanned the area. A security guard stood next to the register, chatting with the cashier. Two older women who stood a few feet behind chatted about celebrating their winnings over a drink. A talk, dark and handsome man, about Emilee's age, caught her eye from across the way. He smiled at her. She smiled back and coyly looked away. When she looked back in his direction, the man was gone.

At the counter, Emilee purchased a medium coke and a bottle of water (for her mother, just in case). As she walked back to the Joker's Wild slot machines, a man approached her.

"Hello."

"Hi," she replied. It was the same man she had spotted earlier.

"You are beautiful."

"Oh, thanks," Emilee replied kindly. Talk, dark and handsome looked even better up close. "What's your name?"

"Robert. Friends call me Rob. Look, my friend wanted me to give this to you."

Robert handed Emilee a card.

Emilee looked confused. "But I thought…"

"I'm sorry. I'm married. My friend over there wanted you to have this."

Emilee glanced over to see a tall, strange looking man smiling back at her. He was sitting at a slot machine just feet away from her mother. Emilee reviewed the business card Robert handed to her: DJ QUICK, 786-444-3251.

DJ Quick was interested in Emilee.

Disgusted, Emilee walked back over to her mother. As she arrived, the men approached Brenda too, Robert… and the famous DJ Quick.

With chart topping hits for some of the world's greatest artists, DJ Quick became a general household name. What's more was his savory appetite for young, naïve women who were more interested in his wallet than his horrid personality and looks. He built a reputation for womanizing and heartbreaking that preceded him. Knowing all this, Emilee wanted nothing to do with him.

"Hello, miss," DJ Quick greeted Brenda.

"Hello, I know who you are!" Brenda remarked.

"Is this pretty lady your daughter?" He asked.

"Yes, she is. Her name is Emilee," Brenda offered.

"Well, I want to ask her out."

"She's a grown woman. She can speak for herself. Baby?" Brenda nudged.

"No, I'm good. Let's go, Ma," Emilee responded.

"It's all good. Damn, you're fine," DJ Quick said. Robert smiled. They watched the women walk away.

Weeks later, Emilee was at South Dade indoor flea market. The flea market was open weekly from Wednesday through Sunday and offered a variety of vendors, including hair and nail salon services. Emilee liked the work of one vendor, Sulie's Nail Salon. She and Sulie, the owner, became friends. As a result, Emilee became one of Sulie's VIP customers. As Emilee entered the salon, she caught the heavy smell of nail polish and other chemicals. She sat in Sulie's chair as Sulie began cutting the cuticles.

"So what have you been up to lately?" Sulie inquired.

"The usual… school, my son, work," Emilee said.

"How about a new man? A pretty girl like you should be hitched."

"I'm still waiting for the one," Emilee added.

The women chatted for about 45 minutes, more than enough time for Emilee's nails to dry fully. Next was Emilee's hair, which required a touch up. Sulie relocated her client to another chair where her hair was cut, styled, and set.

"I'll be right back," Sulie said and disappeared to tend to her business operations.

Emilee surveyed the area. Families bustled about shopping the vendor booths. Sulie's Salon played the best music. Emilee registered the song playing, "Love" by Keyshia Cole.

"Miccosukee…" said a voice in the distance.

Emilee frowned. Who on earth could possess such a name?

"Miccosukee…" said the voice again, this time coming closer, just behind Emilee.

"Miccosukee! Red girl. I'm talking to you…" continued the voice, this time, just a foot away.

Then he appeared.

DJ Quick made his way into Emilee's view. He stood there with the same ugly smile he had on his face back when they first met at the gaming resort.

"At least you could remember my name," Emilee responded. "Leave me alone!"

Disappointed, DJ Quick walked way.

"He should have remembered my name," Emilee thought. "Men are like stray cats. Feed them once… they'll keep coming back."

Near the Shore's Edge

*S*HE SMILED. HER face radiated a light that beckoned me.

I saw her from time to time. Her beauty sculpted like a goddess'. Her waist just the right hourglass shape and those wide firm hips… a baby maker's delight. She was just my height too when she wore heels. Her breasts were the perfect cup size.

I loved everything about her… those deep, hazel eyes and shoulder-length hair with accents of gray and brunette. She epitomized perfection. Her name was Ashley. I didn't know her last name at first. I was destined to make her my baby's mama.

For two weeks, she and I never even spoke. I watched her from a distance from my usual spot at the bar. Seven seats over from her left and adjacent from the bartender's tip jar. Men and women too would try to woo her. She would kindly decline their advances. The more I watched her, the more I wanted her.

Sometimes, when I was alone in my bed, I'd fantasize about her. She'd be sleeping in the blank space to my right just after lovemaking.

I imagined her sexiness pouring from every fiber of her body. I wouldn't touch her. Instead I'd just stare and smile and remain grateful that such a treasure was mine to have.

Finally, we spoke after two weeks. She looked my way. I gazed at her and smiled. She smiled. She motioned me to join her on the empty barstool to her right. I got nervous, yet I persevered.

"I've noticed you sitting over there looking at me for a while," she began.

I froze again. My dreams were fading. She probably thinks I'm a weirdo.

"But it's cool. I'm Ashley. Nice to meet you…"

"Ronald," I said. "Friends call me Ron. Nice to meet you, Ashley."

"What brings you here?" she inquired.

"Work related stress and a need for relief," I responded.

And then there was an awkward silence. Did I say something wrong? Great job, Ron. You ruined another opportunity again with your sarcasm.

"Me, too." She added. "Life can be a piece of work."

"Yeah, I agree."

And we chatted for two hours about our lives. She was born in Ft. Lauderdale and I in Homestead. Her parents were both college educated and sent her to the finest private schools. I told her how I grew up poor and lived in government housing. Her parents were instrumental in her life story. Mine could care less, but somehow I made it. We were polar opposites, and that wasn't good.

But there was an unspoken energy that connected us. It was something more than just sexual, which was obvious, too. She represented a truth that I had to have and wanted to remain in my life. How could I have feelings for someone I barely knew and fantasized about? The more she spoke, the more I wanted to explore her. Man, I got to find a hobby.

Our conversation was very refreshing. Not only was she a beauty, but she was an intellect too. Ashley talked about her latest book club reading, *A Reluctant Fundamentalist*. She recounted the story's plot, an arranged meeting of an unknown Indian protagonist and his experiences in an unfamiliar American culture. Somewhere in the conversation, she mentioned the word *reluctant* a few times. *Reluctant* was how I felt when she first asked me to join her. For two weeks, I watched her ward off unwanted advances. But that night, she chose me.

The night was coming to an end. I realized it was getting late and I had to work early in the morning.

"Gosh, I never do this, but I feel really comfortable talking to you, Ron."

I admitted the same. I hadn't felt that good after a conversation since I divorced my ex five years before.

"Lock my number in your phone. Ready?" Ashley prompted.

"Sure."

"305-726…"

I typed in the number and texted her back. She pulled out a phone that was ringing from inside her purse. I-Phone lover… my kind of girl.

I walked her to her car. As we walked she spoke further about her life. Ashley loved kids but didn't want any of her own. Coming from a large family, she didn't need the stress of raising kids. She cajoled that she could borrow her sister's kids whenever she wanted. But if her future husband ever wanted them, she'd consider it.

We finally reached her car, carbon-colored BMW Series 5. I was impressed. The car's color matched the dark mystery hidden in her beauty. It was a majestic vehicle for a stunning goddess. This lady had class and substance. This was the type of woman you bring home to mama.

Then Ashley and I started going out. I took her to my favorite restaurant, *Soyka*, near the Wynwood District. She was a conscientious eater, ordering the large garden salad with grilled chicken. I kept up with her by ordering healthily too. We enjoyed one another's company for four hours. Ashley worked for a major commercial realtor and was pretty good at what she did. I chatted about my corporate directorship in the HR department for a national law firm.

We both were committed to our work and successful all the same. Yet we both had something that the other needed...

Companionship. We were single and quite lonely at times. By week two Ashley confessed how she longed for companionship and was grateful I was there to give it to her.

One night, as I dropped her off at her condo, she paused and looked over at me.

"Gosh, Ron. I don't know what to say."

"About what?" I asked.

"Everything. These past two weeks have been amazing. I can't thank you enough." Ashley's smile melted my heart.

"No need to. You've made me feel good too."

"Would you like to come up?" She invited.

"Sure."

An hour later, I'm in bed with her; we're both naked. Not only was the sex phenomenal, but so was the post-intimacy. Ashley wasn't like those women who want to cuddle, which I didn't mind. She stared up at the ceiling with a big grin on her face. We chatted more about life.

"You know," she began. "I could get use to having you around."

"Really?" I asked.

"Yeah, you're a good guy. You're good-looking and have a lot to offer. What gives?"

"I've been waiting for you, Ashley," I responded. She hoisted herself up to my face with her elbows and looked into my eyes. Our gazes locked. For a brief moment, there were no words... just glances. Those eyes peered into me in ways no other set had done. She had officially won me over.

And she planted the most sensuous kiss on my lips. It wasn't a French kiss or anything overly sexual. It was a passionate, appreciative kiss that confirmed her feelings. I held her tightly as we continued to make out.

Who could ask for anything more? Ashley was the one for me.

Five years later, Ashley and I bought our first home together. We both wanted a house that had a vintage, Southern charm with hints of the contemporary world. We were fortunate to find and seize a good deal in Coral Gables. The association fees were astronomical, but the scenery just lovely. The house was a three-two with an in-law quarter unit in the back. A large palm tree stood at the edge that separated our yard from our neighbor's. A mango tree grew in the backyard and provided plenty of tropical smoothie drinks to our morning's delight.

Ashley was up early that morning. She insisted on cleaning the house even when we could afford to hire someone else to do it. She was still dressed in her workout clothing when we met up at the kitchen counter.

"Got some news you could use, babe," she started.

"What's up?" I asked. I was still a bit groggy from waking up.

"My sister, Pauline, is coming to town."

"Okay," then I sighed. Pauline and I didn't get along as well as we'd hope.

"I want you two to get along. Sometimes you carry on like a brother and sister. I know it's love… over me." She chuckled.

"That's true, but the woman offers an opinion in times when she really shouldn't. She needs to know her place."

"She's also a widow. Give her time." Ashley added.

"But her husband died ten years ago."

"So what? Some people need more time to get over a loss."

"But life is for the living, Ash. She has to find a way to move on."

"Damn it!" Ashley exclaimed. "Sometimes you can be so insensitive."

I was flustered. I didn't mean to fight with her, but an early morning discussion about her sister didn't appeal to me in the slightest.

"Look," I started, "I'm not here to fight about Pauline. She's family and I love her. Let's change the subject."

By now, I was fully awake. I looked sincerely at Ashley's menacing eyes.

"Fine, she'll be here at 6 p.m." Ashley stated as she walked briskly out of the kitchen.

We took Pauline to dinner at the *Red Fish Grill*. The restaurant featured fine dining with healthy seafood options. Pauline brought her friend, Belkys, with her. The four of us sat on the veranda near the water. Thought it was getting dark, we could still see the waves beating heavily upon the coastline. The place wasn't too crowded that night. In fact, the environment was quite intimate. For a brief moment, I wish it were just Ashley and I in that moment.

We talked about family affairs. Pauline's son, Christopher, had just graduated from the University of Florida. He was scouting graduate schools with the University of Miami being a lead potential. Somewhere in the conversation, Pauline suggested that Christopher move in with us while he attended school.

"It don't want to impose," Pauline mentioned.

"Well," Ashley started, looking over at me. "We have to discuss things first."

"Well, Ron, you like my son, don't you?" Pauline stated.

"What kind of a question is that, Pauline. You know he means the world to me. He's like a son to me."

"Then it's settled. I'll let Chris know."

I got up and walked beyond the veranda's edge. I started out at the water.

"Go talk to him, Pauline." Ashley insisted. Hesitantly, Pauline walked over to me.

At first, we said nothing. I stared out into the darkening coast. I couldn't stand to look at her. I could feel her standing there and looking at me.

"Sorry," Pauline said.

I remained silent. Standing there near the shore's edge, I yearned for a way out of our conversation.

"We have to stop carrying on like this."

"Like what?" I asked.

"This game!" A couple sitting nearby looked our way. I shushed her.

"You know why I act this way," I retorted.

"And it doesn't have to be this way." Pauline replied, trying to sound comforting.

"She doesn't have to know," I concluded.

I turned to look at Pauline.

"I know, Ron. But this is too much. Chris is your son too."

I walked away from her, just like I walked away from him 24 years ago. My life was complete. I had all I needed and had rebound from turmoil. Of all the storylines to read, why did mine have to end with strife? I mean, should I be punished for my past mistakes? And my wife, my lovely, beautiful wife. How would she feel learning that her sister was my one-night stand when we were in college? Could she fathom this? Could she bear to be with a man who had abandoned his son and scarred her sister for the rest of her life?

I returned to the table, leaving Pauline standing there… in tears.

T.H.O.T.

*T*HE SQUARE WAS a place where retired teachers and employed district administrators hung out and shot the breeze. Located in the heart of Liberty City, the building was about 800 square feet, just large enough for a small bar and a few stools to match. Max, the owner, owned the establishment for nearly 30 years. In its heyday, it was a fine place for Happy Hours and meeting sophisticated people. Unfortunately, it became a "hole in the wall" and "rumormongering arena" for all sorts of crap. The place smelled like cigarettes and old cabbage. But people who frequented the spot didn't go for its four-star features. They went to get into trouble or to talk about it.

Robert frequented the Square on a weekly basis. By day, he served as a department chair at an inner city high school. At night, he was an occassional Square patron, taking refuge there with a case of beer he toted to share with his comrades. Standing five feet, six inches and with a slight beer belly, Robert could easily be mistaken for a white preacher man who acted black, at least by black standards. Hints of gray hair accented his temples and mustache. After two unsuccessful marriages, Robert had created a barrier between love and him. He fathered children, three to be exact, who could barely stand him. So the Square was a great place to *let loose.*

Robert's causasian colleagues could not understand his fascination to hang out in in the hood. For nearly 30 years, he made the Square his second home. According to his second ex-wife, the Square ruined their relationship. She said that he chose hanging out there over spending time with her and the kids. Robert dismissed her claims and stated they grew apart. Or rather, she grew apart from him and what they had.

But the truth was…

Robert was alone.

After his second divorce, he vowed never to return home to an empty apartment where silence whispered to him from every corner. When he was in his 40's, silence was a welcomed guest. Nearing 60, it was the guest that outstayed its welcome. Silence invited depression to the apartment on occasion. They liked to tag team Robert, and he despised that. When his mother fell ill, he invited her to stay with him until her dying day. That was an okay time though it wasn't perfect. Constant checkups and hospital visits eventually led to chemo. Finally, it was all over. His mother's departure wasn't what tormented him, but the possibility of dying alone did. But Robert's relationship track record wasn't all that appealing either.

When the final bell rang that Friday, Robert was the first teacher out of the building and in the parking lot. It was a payday too. Walking to his car, he ran into his colleague.

"Heading over to the Square?" Francisco asked.

He pushed the button on his car's remote to unlock the doors. His car was parked right next to Robert's.

"Yep, I am," Robert said. He unlocked the car door.

"Be careful and lay off the happy sauce," Francisco warned, referring to Robert's liquor intake.

"Yeah, yeah, whatever. You know I'm stupid," Robert commented.

He got in his car, turned the key in the ignition and eventually drove away.

His 2005 Nissan Ultima was still in decent condition though it needed some work. His mechanic suggested that he buy new tires and change the spark plugs within the next month. These things were important, but not as important to supplying his appetite for happy sauce. He made a quick stop at the local Winn Dixie to pick up a case of Coronas, the 18-case set. The man rarely ate a wholesome meal; the beer served him plenty. Averaging three cases a week, Robert's version of a liquid diet rewarded him with bouts of abdominal pains and shortness of breath. He recently developed a cough that would shake his students and peers. He hated doctors, so he elected not to visit them.

The Square was busy on Friday. The weather was hot and humid and the mosquitos were hungry... a typical summer night in Miami.

There were no parking spaces left. People began to park on the curb and the sidewalks of the neighborhood houses that were across the street from the Square. Some neighbors were smart. They placed sizeable, pyramid-shaped cement blocks outside their homes to block potential parkers. Fortunately, Robert knew Uncle Jack, a resident of one of the homes. He and Robert formed a bond years back, resulting in Robert gaining full access to park anytime on Uncle Jack's property. Robert pulled into the driveway, put the car in park, and then got out. Popping the trunk, he secured his wheeled cooler. He and his happy sauce were soon crossing the street to join his comrades at the Square.

Since the establishment provided its own beer, Robert wasn't allowed to bring his inside. Instead he pulled the cooler over to an outdoor spot: a tall tree. He pulled up an available chair and opened his cooler to grab a beer. Uncle Jack noticed his arrival and went over to greet Robert; other patrons, Johnny and Spot, greeted them.

"Good to see you, Rob, how's it going?" Uncle Jack asked.

"It's Friday... and a pay Friday. It's all good," Robert replied.

"Any freaks on the list this weekend, Rob?" Spot asked. He was the Square idiot.

"Nah, not this weekend. Got child support to pay," Robert said.

"Man, when you done with that? How old is your kid?" Johnny inquired.

"Almost 18."

"Damn, you gotta cut those shackles off and start living. Better be saving for retirement too," Johnny said.

"Yeah, yeah… hey, look at this," Robert said. He pulled out his Samsung cellphone and opened the picture app. He chose one picture, zoomed in on it, and passed it around the group.

"Damn!" Johnny exclaimed. "Who dem belong to?"

"Dem some big ass meat curtains!" Spot yelled.

Everyone laughed. Robert showed them naked pictures of a prospect.

"If you don't want 'em, I'll take 'em," Johnny approved. He licked his lips as he gazed at the pic. "Text that pic to me."

"Nope, all mine, man. You're married. What would your wife say?" Robert asked.

"What she don't know won't hurt her," Johnny assured.

Everyone laughed. The liquor began to settle in. Robert was relaxed and having a good time.

Two hours passed and more people arrived. Robert knew everyone by name. Moses, the preacher at the local church, had stopped by in hopes of converting Square sinners into congregation goers. Rex, a retired music teacher, was Uncle Jack's cousin. He grew up across the street from the Square, watching the drama from his family's porch. He dropped in primarily for business reasons. His son, Tim, accompanied him. Tim grew up a few blocks away as well. People said he made his money hustling or pimping. No one knew how he could afford to wear expensive fitted caps and sneakers, or how he could afford to drive a limited edition Mercedes. When he dropped in, drinks were free. He spotted the tab.

Tim sat by Robert. Robert smiled. Tim was Robert's high school student a decade before. The young man had grown taller than Robert could remember. His chiseled frame looked menacing. His forearms were tatted up. Over the years, he and Robert formed a friendship. He knew Robert's desires and gave him gifts from time to time.

"Thanks for the tip," Robert began.

"You're welcome. So you like her, huh?" Tim asked.

"I do, and the guys liked her pic, too," Robert said.

"You showed her pics to these men?" Tim asked, looking around the area. "These men are all horny for what you got. Don't fuck it up."

"I won't," Robert said. "Where is she, anyway?"

"She's here… That hoe over there…" Tim said, gesturing toward the THOT.

Twenty feet away, Robert spotted her. Standing near the sidewalk, just where the Square's tree hangout ended, was a dark, fine lady.

Shanice was dressed in the finest ratchet wear. Her tall, slender legs stretched for days. Her round butt matched her firm legs perfectly. She wore a tight-fitted tank top with the number 21 bedazzled in sequins. Her laced-front wig ran down her back in dark raven waves. The woman was pretty. Her three-year-old son was next to her. Both of them stood out like sour thumbs. A chick like her and her child were uncommon at the Square.

Robert fell instantly in love. Every step Shanice took toward him, he was mesmerized. Strangely enough, her breasts didn't match the meat curtains featured in the phone pic. Perhaps there was a mix-up.

"You sure that's the same girl? She's not fat," Robert said to Tim.

"It's her. She lost a lot of weight after her second kid," Tim said.

"You mean there's another one? Shit," Robert said.

"Yep, that one is her first," Tim said.

Shanice greeted Tim with a hug. They were work associates after all.

"This is Robert." Robert and Shanice's eyes met. He grinned. She smiled. Love was in the air.

One week later, he moved her and the two kids into his bachelor pad. She was an unemployed high school dropout. When she and the kids arrived, his place reeked of garbage and musk. After two days, Shanice had the place squeaky clean. She gave it a thorough scrub. She removed the shower curtain liners and bleach-washed them. She dusted ceiling fans and purged old clothing in the master closet. Even though she was a hood rat, she still enjoyed a quality living space. Robert's two-bed, two-bath apartment became her new home.

Robert became the kids' father figure. On weekends, they went as a family to the Aventura Mall, to window shop. Robert carried the little girl in the child harness strapped to his back. The little boy and mom walked hand and hand. He would buy the kid ice cream. In exchange, Shanice would give him *some* later that evening. The four of them made a perfectly abnormal family. It had nothing to do with their racial difference… but everything to do with… well, everything.

The next morning, Shanice had prepared a fine breakfast for Robert and the kid. Scrambled eggs and toast with grape jelly and a glass of orange juice. Robert rarely had time to make breakfast. Usually, his breakfast and lunch consisted of a quart of black coffee in a rarely washed thermos. That day, he ditched the thermos.

Shanice fed the boy. The baby slept still.

"I want you to stop going to the Square," she requested.

"What?" he asked.

"You heard me. It's not good for you. We're a family now. Come home."

"I can't do that," he said.

"Why not?" Shanice asked.

"I can't," was all he said. He got up from the table and headed out for work.

At the end of the workday, Robert was back at the Square. Uncle Jack and Johnny were already there. They chose to sit inside at the bar. Miami's unpredictable weather brought infrequent downpours followed by rays of torrid sunshine. As the men drank and talked, the downpour pounded the roof. Thunder rumbled in the distance.

"And you moved her in?" Johnny inquired.

"Yeah, yeah, I did. She's getting too serious. I'm not ready for that," Robert responded.

"Be careful with that THOT, man," Uncle Jack warned. "You know she used to live in a halfway house with 'dem kids."

"I didn't know that," Robert said. He swigged his Corona.

"Well, everyone does. Be careful," Uncle Jack said.

"But she got the nicest pu…." Robert began, smiling.

"Man, fuck that! Don't catch nothin' you can't get rid of," Johnny suggested in an excited tone.

He rocked back and forth on his stool, trying to contain himself. He got jittery when he learned something juicy.

"She moved her friend in, Bernice," Robert confessed. Bernice was unemployed too.

"Another THOT? Man, let me get one," Johnny exclaimed.

"You're running your own halfway house, man," Uncle Jack said. "Clean your house out."

"I know, I'm stupid," Robert admitted.

Women have it hard, it seems. In the world, there are two types of men: Men who are responsible and men who never grow up, the man-child. Robert had become one, a man-child, incapable of living his life fully without the inclusion of ghetto drama and other immaturities. At his age, you would expect him to know better. But loneliness and depression had already moved into his place well before Shanice and her kids had arrived. Uncle Jack was right. That condo was packed with crap he needed to toss.

"I'm stupid," Robert repeated. "For once, I feel like Spot."

"Well, there's a difference between you and Spot," Johnny said. "Spot don't shit where he eats."

"You got that woman coming to your job?" Uncle Jack asked.

"She drops me off and sometimes helps me grade papers, that's all," Robert said.

"You're cruisin' for a bruisin', man. Tighten up!" Uncle Jack scolded.

Uncle Jack looked seriously at Robert who ignored him. Uncle Jack was like a father figure to Robert. Robert was Uncle Jack's prodigal son.

Later that night, Bernice came on to Robert. At first, he tried to resist her advances, but then he eventually succumbed to them. Ultimately, it was what he wanted. An older white male caught in a love triangle with two deranged, young black women.

Shanice and the kids were sleeping in the master bedroom. Bernice wasn't as pretty as Shanice, but she had the type of meat curtains that Robert liked. They kissed passionately in the kitchen, away from the doorway entrance facing the master bedroom. Her breath smelled like Amoretto, arousing him. They consummated their indiscretions on the kitchen table, stove, and everywhere in between while Shanice slept soundly.

In two weeks, two women walked into Robert's life. One week thereafter, Shanice left, but not without a fight.

She showed up at the high school with a bat and a promise. Robert avoided her calls. She called around to his friends and co-workers and even popped up at the Square, looking for her him. But she didn't have a car to make it to his place. She didn't have a penny to her name but those two kids. Somehow, she showed up to the school with her mother, kids and aunt in the car. They watched from the car.

"Robert Jeffries, this is for you!" She yelled.

Shanice was dressed for the occasion. She wore tight shorts, a shower cap, and a halter-top, exposing her firm stomach. She wore no makeup and earrings. Shanice was ready to scrap.

She started smashing his car like a mad woman. She went to work on the windshield, which cracked instantly under her assault. Her actions drew a crowd. Francisco and his students came out of their woodshop area to witness the action. Students pulled out their cellphones and some started to shout "World Star." The spectacle attracted a campus security officer who patrolling the area in a golf cart. Moments later, a police car arrived. Shanice was arrested and taken to the county jail.

Bernice and Robert dated for another month. The school principal asked Robert to take a few days off to get his life in order. He and Shanice traveled to Port St. Lucie to visit Robert's elderly father, who stayed in an assisted living facility.

Robert introduced Bernice as his new girlfriend. The old man smiled at them both. Consummation at last. Another man and his THOTS...oops, thoughts.

It Was about Me

I WAS AN OPTIMIST. I tried to see things from all sides. But there was one thing I could not tolerate, and that was bullshit.

Friendships were hard to come by. You had to invest in them to make them work. For the past 30 years, I invested in people who I thought were friends… attending destination weddings at my expense, going to extravagant birthdays for a one-year old who won't remember it (other than by pictures), and taking midnight trips to the E-R with a friend's significant other who I barely knew…and what did I have to show for this?

I had it made, living on Brickell. I had a nice bachelor pad with a gorgeous water view. If you looked just south from my balcony, on a clear summer night, you'd see the Miami Seaquarium's octagonal structure in the distance. Warm air brought a musty-sweet smell of sea salt from the ocean's waves. My studio was pretty spacious and contemporary. The investor wanted a place that attracted young professionals and international travellers alike. Well, he sold me.

Work was a ten-minute walk from my building. My office was just north of my building. I worked for one of the most prominent international law firms in the nation. Even though I'd only been employed for five years, it was where I wanted to be for the rest of my life, at least professionally. My office was on the 19th floor with a window view. Some days when I looked down on the street from that window, all I could see were colorful spots moving. From above, I just saw moving specs. A closer look revealed the truth... and an epiphany.

I wished that I had somewhere to go.

I came from a good family and attended Florida International University then the University of Miami. I always had a plan. Originally, I wanted to move away to Manhattan and build my life there. That would have been somewhere to go. Or maybe I could have moved to the West Coast and worked for a firm that represents folks in Silicon Valley. Being placed in good circumstances was not always a good thing. I was missing something...

Love.

Or lust, or a girl. Wait, maybe a woman. Someone who I could call at noon on Fridays and arrange a Happy Hour date with co-workers. I wouldn't mind sharing my space with her, either. After Happy Hour, I would head over to the Capital Grille for dinner. I hoped she liked those places as much as I do. If not, we would head north to the inner streets of Downtown Miami and try Fritelli's Italian Restaurant. The food and ambiance were that good. I couldn't help it. I was a romantic.

Later, we would return to my place and star gaze. I imagined her standing on the balcony and peering into the darkness. I would approach her behind and grab her waist. She would turn to kiss me, but I would hold her in place. It wasn't about the lip locking and passionate lovemaking. It had to start with a connection, a mental and spiritual connection. She would be the one and I'd give my heart to her completely.

I closed my eyes.

I could feel the warmth of her body against me. The humid breeze from the sea touched us. She snuggled into me. Something stirred in my groin. It was bound to be a good night…

I opened my eyes.

I was in my office. Shit! The whole time I had been daydreaming in my fucking office.

The door opened. Laura, the office manager, entered.

"The deposition is ready, Miguel", she said handing me the file.

"Thanks," I said. I was still out of it. Laura smiled. For the first time, I noticed her beautiful teeth, pearly white and perfect.

"I'm about to leave. Is there anything else I can do for you?" She asked.

"There is…" I began.

Laura looked at me, waiting for a response.

"Forget it," I added.

"You sure?" Laura asked. She looked puzzled.

"Yeah, I'm good. Have a great night."

"You too," I said.

I knew I should never shit where I ate. I'd never done it, but I knew friends who had. Dating co-workers was risky and unprofessionalism. I knew Laura for a few years and never realized how pretty she was until then.

I decided to head over to Capital Grill for a party of one. I ordered my favorite entrée, the grilled salmon with steamed veggies and brown rice. A glass of white wine accompanied the meal. I sipped the wine slowly. The Chardonnay tasted good and paired well with the fish. I scanned the room. Most people were in groups of twos or threes. I was sitting alone. Most times, it didn't bother me, but that night was different.

"Sir," the waiter called. He was holding something. "Compliments of the patron at the bar."

I looked over at the bar, which was less than ten feet away. An older man and his wife chatted away. They weren't even looking my way. Nearby, two women made a toast. Moments later, two other women joined them. They were hot too. But none of them were looking my way.

Then I saw a man sitting at the end of the bar. He looked about my age. He tipped his glass toward me and smiled. I frowned… not interested.

I returned to my plate. I had only eaten half of it. And I dared not look again in the direction of that guy. What did he want from me? I quickly glanced his way, but he was gone.

"Miguel?" A voice asked. It came from behind me.

That guy made his way to my table.

"Do I know you?" I started. I wasn't interested in what he was selling.

"I'm Derrick. We met last year during the Gonzalez vs. Velazquez case. You worked for the defending team."

Suddenly, it hit me. Derrick was on the prosecuting team for that case, and we had won. As a reward, my boss offered me a bonus and an all-paid expenses week in Tahiti. Derrick and I had our chance at the bench, each delivering what we were expected to.

"I come in peace, Miguel. We had a few, good laughs afterwards, remember?" he reminded.

"I do," I said. I paused for a moment. The guy is just being nice. "Okay, would you like to join me?"

"Thank you," he replied.

For an hour, we spoke about our firms and our future goals. Derrick wanted to start his own national firm. Ironically, he and I were both Miami-born Cubans. His father arrived in Miami during the Mariel boatlift. His life story sounded like a movie with the traditional rags-to-riches plotline. An Ivy League college graduate, Derrick could write his ticket to go anywhere and everywhere he wanted. I envied that.

He said he was in town for a few days visiting family before heading to Los Angeles. I drank his complimentary glass of wine and asked for another. Three glasses later, I was feeling really good. Derrick had a few more too.

Later, we ended up at my place. I wasn't drunk but far from being totally sober. Derrick relaxed on my couch, and we were listening to music playing through my wireless home theatre speakers. Drake's "Hotline Bling" blares throughout the room. Feeling silly, I got up and imitated Drake's moves from the music video. Derrick laughed. Moments later, he joined me, and we were both acting like fools.

"I can't remember when I had this much fun, man," I said. I collapse back on the couch.

"Neither can I," Derrick admitted.

"Hotline Bling" ended and Adele's "Hello" began.

"Hello?" Derrick mocked.

"Is it me you're looking for?" I sang.

"Wrong song, man. You're out of it," he said, chuckling. He rested his head back on the couch and looked over at me.

I stared at him. For the first time, I noticed his dark brown eyes. There was a spark of hope in them. He had facial hair, like me. His nose was slightly pointed.

"Come here," I beckoned.

We walked over to the balcony. I opened the balcony door and stepped out onto the surface. Derrick followed. The warm night air greeted us.

"This is awesome, Miguel," Derrick said while scanning the outer distance.

A crescent moon hung high in the sky. I heard the faint sounds of marine life combined with the sounds of waves meeting the shoreline. Derrick walked over to the railing and leaned. He folded his hands in front of him. I joined him, standing to his left. We stared out into the night.

"I dream about being here with someone special," I confessed.

"Oh, yeah? With who?" Derrick asked.

"No one in particular."

"Hmm," he said.

He looked over at me and smiled. I smiled.

I felt weird. Something strange was happening. Talking to Derrick felt good. He seemed to understand where I was coming from even though we had known each other for a very a short time.

Derrick inched over to me.

He nudged me out of my spot. I moved over to let him stand in my place. Almost naturally, I assumed the position behind him. We stood there, on the balcony, holding each other and staring into the darkness.

I didn't know what had happened or why it happened. I thought about life and how fickle it could be. We humans weren't programmed to be alone. So it didn't matter how we enjoyed our company.

Derrick and I didn't sleep together.

But we were emotionally connected. It felt good, and I'd do it again. Maybe it was about me. Or maybe it was the way it was supposed to be.

Fuck Boy's Transformation

"LITTLE BROTHER, I got news for you… women EXPECT you to treat them like shit," Donald said as he examined himself one last time in the bathroom mirror.

Carlos, watched from the doorway. He held on to every word Donald said.

"Ultimately, you want to bang her, but she may not be ready for it. That's when you wait," Donald added, turning to face Carlos. "How do I look, bruh?"

Carlos gave him a thumbs up. Donald's striped crimson and white polo and designer jeans were classic. He wore a fitted, raven-colored New York Yankees cap. His white Nikes, Fossil watch and belt completed the set. To many Donald was a label whore. But to Carlos, he was an urban legend.

"I can't wait to go to the clubs with you, Don," Carlos said. "You have it all."

"Yeah, I do," Donald agreed. "And ain't nobody gonna take from me what's meant for me. You feel me?"

"Yep, I do," Carlos said.

Carlos followed him downstairs to the living room.

Faint smells of *arroz con pollo* waivered in the air from the nearby kitchen. On the couch sat Boo, Donald's Tuxedo cat. With its yellow eyes, Boo watched Donald search the couch for his cellphone. Donald discovered it buried between the thick cushions, almost invisible. He pressed the home key and saw three missed calls, each from someone he was supposed to meet up with later that evening. It was 10:48 p.m., still early by clubbing standards. Donald pocketed his cellphone.

"Another lesson," he continued, "Never let 'em know you're in route… just show up fashionably late. Everyone will notice you."

As he passed the couch, Donald petted Boo on the head. Of all the family members in the house, Boo desired Donald's affection the most. Yet Donald engaged with Boo the least. Even after Donald had rescued Boo from his best friend's litter of newborn kittens, Carlos was the one who took care of the cat and provided all that it needed. However, Carlos didn't mind taking care of his brother's cat. It gave him a chance to be closer to his idol even if Donald didn't notice it.

"Don't wait up for me," Donald reminded as he walked out the front door and onto the porch.

The night air was humid and stifling. Donald adjusted his cap and walked toward his parked car, a midnight blue Camaro. In the dark, no one could really distinguish its actual color for it looked so majestic. It was a gift from their parents on Donald's 21st birthday. Six months later, the car was still in good condition surprisingly and had avoided a major accident. Donald named the car "Duchess." He treated that car better than most of the women he dated.

Eventually, Donald was in his Camero and pulling out of the driveway. He could see Carlos in the rearview mirror as he drove away.

Thirty minutes later on the other side of town, Donald valeted his Camero and approached the building. Club Space's entrance beckoned him in. The house music blared loudly through the door every time the bouncers opened it to grant VIP access. Donald approached the first bouncer, a solid, tall Afro-Cuban man with biceps as big as Donald's head. Their eyes met. Not a word was said. Minutes later, Donald was inside thumping to the beat of the club's music lounge.

DJ Obscene was spinning live. The place was packed from wall to wall and smelled like chronic and a newly constructed building. Neon strobe lights bounced on every wall. The temperature was warm. Tight gym bodies and petite waists were everywhere. It was hard to make out any familiar faces among the masses. Donald headed toward the VIP lounge.

Tino and Marcos were waiting for him, each with a drink in one hand and a cellphone in the other. Both were so occupied with their latest Snapchat posts that they didn't see Donald approaching. They were too enthralled in their mobile phones.

"What up!" Donald greeted.

Both men stopped their posting and greeted their friend in typical machisimo fashion, the *fist bump*… the contemporary handshake.

"Man, this place is lit!" Tino commented, trying to communicate with his friends above the sound of the loud music.

"Some cute bitches in here. And one of them is mine!" Marcos added.

"I need a drink. What you drinking?!" Donald asked.

"Man, the only one I know, Patron!!!" Tino responded, passing the half-empty bottle to Donald.

"I got next round, for sure!" Donald offered.

The night was still young.

About an hour later, the club was packed with even more bodies. Word on the floor was that the building had reached its capacity. Bouncers guarded the front door like it was a medieval fortress. Dj Obscene was spinning a remix of the latest tracks. The crowd went wild. As the sound increased, the liquor kept coming. Round two drinks were ordered.

"Hey, that girl keeps eying you, man," Tino said, gesturing toward two women standing near the VIP lounge.

"Which one?" Donald asked.

"That one, the one with the thick ass and long hair. Look at that ass!" Tino exclaimed. "If you don't want her, I'll take her."

The young woman looked in Donald's direction. Through the strobe lights and shadows, he could faintly make out her face, but knew she indeed looked in his direction.

"Hey, baby!" Tino exclaimed as he approached the women.

"Babies don't come this big, papi," the taller woman replied.

"Damn, so it's like that?" Tino asked.

"My friend wanted to say hi to your boy over there," the woman responded, looking Donald's way.

All eyes turned to Donald, who was standing with a big smile on his face. As the ladies walked by, Tino and Marcos give them a quick glance over, starting at their faces, down to their breasts, and then to their butts. As the women passed, the men's eyes stayed glued to their bottoms. Tino licked his lips in approval.

"What's your name, cutey?" The taller woman asked. "I'm Gaby and this is my friend Tati."

"A pleasure to meet you both. Drinks?" Donald offered.

"No, thank you," Gaby replied. "I don't drink. But my friend does…" Gaby nudged Tati to speak.

"Girl, I got this! Hello, what's your name?" Tati inquired.

"Donny. You're very pretty. I'm sure you hear this all the time," Donald commented, staring directly into Tati's eyes.

"She does from fuck boys," Gaby chided with a smirk.

"Gaby, stop!" Tati snapped. "Be nice for once."

"Okay, my job is done…" Gaby said, turning toward Tino and Marcos. "I think I'll take that drink now. You buying, playboy?"

Gaby, Tino and Marcos walked away.

Donald and Tati stood face-to-face, each studying the other. She was slightly shorter than he. Her shoulder-length hair contained accents of blond highlights. Her eyes were a stunning deep brown. Despite their dark color, her eyes were soft and inviting. With pouty lips and a small, sculpted nose, Tati possessed a natural beauty. She wore a short dress, revealing two strong, athletic legs. Everything about her made Donald desire her more.

For more than an hour, they talked about growing up in Miami, work, and family. Tati grew up in the heart of Little Havana in a two-bedroom apartment, which housed her, mom, dad, abuelita, and tia. Her plans to start college were delayed after she landed a full-time job working at the post office. For five years, she was able to make a decent living for herself and move out of her mother's place to explore independence. Donald absorbed every word. His eyes never once left hers. The more she spoke, the more he wanted to taste those pouty lips. He imagined what they would taste like. Bubble gum? Cinnamon? Some girls enjoy wearing flavored lip-gloss.

Eventually, they made their way out of Club Space and into the parking lot. Donald opened the passenger door and invited Tati inside. Shortly thereafter, they were on the road.

Donald charmed his way to Tati's place. He followed her into the studio apartment, which was decorated in Ikea exclusives. It was a neat sanctuary, reflecting Tati's personality.

"Would you like another drink?" she offered. Donald nodded.

"This is a nice place, girl. Damn, you rich?" he joked. She chuckled.

"I wish. When I hit the lotto I'll you know."

"I think I hit the lotto by finding you," he flirted.

"Oh, yeah?"

"Yeah."

He gently reached for her hand and brought her into him. Her scent drove him crazy. Their lips locked for the first time.

"Damn, you taste so good too, Mami. I want to get to know you better. You down?" he asked.

"Duh, you're here, aren't you?" she cajoled.

She leaned in for a second kiss. Donald teased her with his fiery tongue. He sampled her lips even again. His hands moved down to the small of her back. He pulled her closer. Both knew what the other wanted and didn't protest.

Tati opened her eyes. The ceiling in her bedroom slowly came into view. The white ceiling fan rotated slowly and quietly. She glanced to her right to discover... an empty space. She sat up. In confusion her eyes searched the room for any trace of her invited guest. His clothes and shoes were gone. His wallet, which he had placed on the nightstand on his side of the bed, was gone too. The man made no attempt to announce his departure. He left her, after getting what he wanted, like a thief in the night.

She walked out to the common area in search of her cellphone. She found it on the couch. The time was 12:48 p.m., Saturday afternoon. The morning had long since passed. She turned to make a cup of coffee when something stopped her in her tracks.

Donald stood there naked and with a large grin. Their eyes met again and she smiled. Her eyes followed the trail of his hair chairs to his waist... then his crotch.

Another hour later, they were spent and resting in her queen-sized bed. For a while, they said nothing to one another. Donald knew that he should have been long gone, but something encouraged him to remain where he was... in her company. Tati strummed his chest hairs with her right fingers. He closed his eyes and smiled. For some reason this chick made him feel comfortable and he liked being in her company.

"This is crazy," she said, breaking the silence.

"What do you mean?" he asked.

"This. Us. Look at us."

"I normally don't do this," he said.

"Neither do I, but I had to... I wanted to... with you," she said slightly gripping his stomach.

"You're cool, Tati. I like being with you."

"Look, I know you're a fuck boy... but..."

"A fuck boy?" he asked with wide eyes.

"Yeah. A fuck boy. But something about you draws me in more. I don't get it," she said.

Donald looked into her eyes. In them he saw hints of hurt, joy, and lust, a hybrid of emotions. But somehow these things were so alluring to him. They were the very things that he lacked in his own persona.

Weeks later, Donald introduced Carlos to his girlfriend Tati; the two immediately connected. The rest of the family met her in time too and they fell in love with Tati.

During dinner one evening, abuelita prophesied that Tati could be the one to bring her great-grandkids.

Carlos and Donald were busily cleaning up the barbeque area in the backyard. Donald scrubbed the grill of charred meat and debris as Carlos folded the picnic table and chairs. The South Florida sun hung lazily in the sky, casting a faint glow on the city.

"Bro, you've changed," Carlos said as he worked.

"What do you mean, man?" Donald asked.

"What happened to all that talk about bitches and pussy?" Carlos countered.

"Yeah, yeah, shut up and put up those damn chairs," Donald replied with a smile. "I forgot to teach you one more lesson."

"What lesson?"

"The one where you ignore your brother when he acts like a fuck boy. You should be better than that."

They looked at one another. Nothing more needed to be said. The fuck boy's transformation was complete.

Lottery Tickets

*M*ARTHA MCCLOUD SAT with her Bible in her lap during Bible study. She was rcsolute and radiant. As a faithful member of the Second Baptist Church in Perrine, Florida, she attended every Wednesday night study session for over twenty years.

Pastor Franklin appreciated Martha's contributions through the years. And recently, because of her efforts, he made her the director of the newly organized youth choir. Martha assured him that she would not let him down. So she busied herself with preparations for the first youth choir production. For an entire week, Martha stayed up well into the night working on the production.

The following Wednesday, she met with the youth group for the initial rehearsal. Hours before, she readied herself for the ultimate task of directing. She photocopied songs from the hymnbook, selecting several selections, "Ride on, King Jesus" and "Who Holds My Hand," church favorites. She was destined to win everyone's approval through her work as choir director.

Dressed in an indigo denim dress and a alabaster sweater, she looked the part. Her naturally kinky hair with hints of blond streaks, fell to her shoulders. She accessorized her ensemble with a gold, Jesus-on-the cross medallion that hung from a 14-karat gold chain. She looked like a God-fearing woman nearing her 50s. Older men at the church still flirted with her every once in a while. The talk of the church was that she was seeing the pastor while still playing friends to his wife.

Yet she possessed a strong spirit; however, her intentions were not always genuine. She knew how to get the job done and she purposely volunteered on numerous projects at the church. Yet she exuded an air of conceitedness about her that irritated other women. She revealed her nastiness in the most opportune times. For instance, when she served on the fundraising committee, the church board knew that she possessed the skills to bring in large donations in a short period of time. Yet no one aired an opinion about her. She was a moneymaker, and the church needed one to keep things moving during financially challenging times.

The youth choir members weren't happy with Marsha's directorship appointment. They knew she could mold them into great singers after enduring harsh and cruel conditions. Charlenia, one of the popular youth soloists, tried to drop the choir after learning of Martha's takeover. Jermaine, the church's top pianist, and top scholar at one of the county's magnet high schools, wanted to get out of "harm's way" as well. Both of the children's parents weren't buying the excuses.

At 6 p.m., Martha walked through the church doors. Under her right arm, she carried her hymnbook and photocopied pages of sheet music. In her left hand was her conductor's baton. Her look was stern and commanded respect. As she approached the group, the children's chattering stopped; their eyes were glued to Martha's every move. Jermaine sat at the piano. He said nothing while eyeing the power-hungry Martha peculiarly. Charlenia shook her head in disbelief. Martha noticed them both and glared at them. She took her place at the director's lectern.

"Good evening, young people. I'm glad you made it," Martha began with a commanding voice. "Tonight, we will be working on harmonizing and learning the words to the hymns I have selected for you. Charlenia, come over and hand these out to everyone."

Charlenia didn't like Martha and she didn't like being her teacher's pet even more. Nevertheless, she passed out the photocopied hymn pages. When she finished, she realized that Martha was short one copy… her own.

"Ms. McCloud, we are short one," said Charlenia, trying to sound polite.

"Then look on with someone else, child. You're a pro," Martha coldly replied.

Charlenia rolled her eyes and returned to her place in the choir.

"Okay, children. Let's find the key. Jermaine, strike the C-note for us."

Looking slightly agitated, Jermaine struck the note.

"No, no! That is not how I want it played, son. Do it again," Martha ranted.

Jermaine struck the note for the second time. Martha was displeased. She tapped her baton on the lectern repeatedly. No one uttered a word or peeped a sound as Martha projected her anger.

"Can't you do this right? What is wrong with you tonight? Did your mother make you mad?!"

Jermaine said nothing.

"Move over!" Martha motioned for Jermaine to stand while she took his place on the piano stool. "This is how it's supposed to sound."

And she struck the note again and again. After what seemed like a minute, she looked back at the youth group.

"Young people, check your attitudes at God's door," she boldly suggested.

Suddenly, someone sucked her teeth.

"Excuse me?!" Martha stood up and faced the group. She jumped up from the piano stool and stood, pouty lipped, with her hands on her hips.

"Who sucked their teeth?"

No one responded.

She suspected heathen kids would cover for each other. She stared them down. If her looks could kill, someone would have dropped dead from all that staring.

The staring match continued for almost five minutes. Martha knew that she had the group right where she wanted it. However, Charlenia looked on, defying Martha's authority with a matching glare of her own.

"Young lady, if you were my daughter, I'd teach you some manners."

"Thank God you are not," Charlenia replied. Two kids snickered.

"Well, when I see your mother, I'll tell her what you said. I wonder what she'd think about your behavior. I'm the adult."

"But it doesn't give you the right to be so mean to people. God doesn't like ugly, Ms. McCloud," Charlenia said. She was fumed.

"I can see this is going to be a long rehearsal. Everyone, take a five-minute break; and when we come back, maybe your attitudes will be less disrespectful."

The group began to retreat to a corner away from Martha. Some kids rolled their eyes as they passed her.

Martha stopped Charlenia in her tracks.

"And Charlenia, remember what I said to you… this is your last warning. Remember… I went to school with your mama."

Charlenia mumbled something under her breath as she walked away.

It took the choir three weeks to learn the songs and sounds on key. Martha worked them like tired mules. During each practice, she grew fiercer and more power hungry. The kids resented her more and more. Many of them complained to their parents, but there was nothing even they could do. Ultimately, Martha wanted absolute sovereignty.

Some parents found the situation peculiar, so they attended the next rehearsal session to see what the talk was all about. On Wednesday night, ten parents piled into the rear of the church hall to watch the rehearsal. Snooty-nosed Martha haughtily reminded them that they were to remain silent during the session.

Charlenia was in front mentally preparing for her solo and the attitude and Martha's attitude. Her peers stood behind her with somber faces.

Martha had robbed the kids of their joy to participate in the church.

She returned to the director's lectern.

She tapped the baton, signaling everyone that she was ready to begin. Charlenia was anxious to get the night over with. Jermaine looked no better. Martha had given him a good scolding several times before he finally found the right key. He struck the key with perfection, just as Martha wanted.

The melodious sounds of the choir rose softly. "Ride on King Jesus" started. Charlenia's soprano voice filled the air. Despite her anger toward Martha, she at least didn't let the woman rob her of her love for God and to sing in his name.

The tempo grew as Jermaine played each note. The choir sang. Each child faked their happiness to be there performing for Martha. With a serious look, Martha conducted the group.

The parents in the back of the church looked on. Some swayed their heads or tapped their feet to the music. They did all this without distracting Martha. In the past, she would stop right in the middle of a practice and reprimand a distractor. She knew how to make parents behave like children too.

After the close-to-four-minute performance, the choir sang its last line and the pianist faded out. Martha put down her baton and looked at the choir sternly.

"Not bad, children." That was her way of saying, "good job."

Then Martha turned to the parents.

"I know you liked that performance."

Shortly afterwards, the kids were taking a break. They congregated toward the back of the church with the parents. Some of them softly chattered. Martha had instructed them to save their voices and their energies for practice and not for gossiping.

Martha knew that some of the whispers and light chatter had to be about her. Charlenia stood toward the center of the group. That scoundrel, Martha thought. Charlenia knew how to win anyone over with her manipulation.

Martha grabbed her Bible and headed over to the group. As she approached, the whispering and chattering ceased.

"I declare onto you and in the name of the Lord that gossip is a sin in every way," she started.

The children and parents just stared at her. They were motionless. They didn't know what to say or do.

"And we will not have that in the house of the Lord tonight!" she continued, yellling as she waived the Bible in the air like a weapon.

The more they stared, the angrier she grew. Her hands were flailing all over the place while still holding the Bible.

"God doesn't like it when His children are distracted with the sinful ways of man! He knows your thoughts and your fears! Surrender to Him all your pain and your sins and He will forgive you! You must do this before it's too late! God doesn't like it when His children are…."

She lost her grip on the Bible. She tried to rescue it to no avail. It fell to the floor; when it hit the floor, all of its contents spilled all over the place.

Several Florida Lottery tickets revealed themselves. Wide-eyed faces and snickering emanated. Martha was harboring a very sinful secret.

Charlenia reached over and picked up one of the scratch-off tickets.

"Ms. McCloud, why do you buy lottery tickets?" The girl asked slyly.

Martha looked stupid. She was speechless. Her eyes scanned the crowd that gathered around her as her sinful act was exposed all around her.

"What? What? Who…" she stuttered.

One of the parents chimed in, "whose are they?"

"They ain't mine!" Martha yelled.

Everyone broke into hysterical laughter.

Martha walked away from the group with the little dignity she had left. For once, she had nothing to say.

If That Sock Could Talk

RAY'S TRIP TO Halloween Horror Nights in Orlando, Florida, was an annual ritual for him and his friends. As usual, the group scheduled to leave late Friday morning and arrive in Orlando by late afternoon. This year's group consisted of seven attendees: Ray, Fabian, Bill, Shanda, Kim, Matt, and David. They all met in college 15 years ago. This trip was their special time to reconnect.

The group decided to caravan to Orlando. Each traveler piled into one of two vehicles, Fabian's 2012 Ford Fusion and David's 2011 Toyota Corolla. It would take them more than three hours to get to their destination, including the occasional bathroom break in Port St. Lucie, the halfway spot between Miami and Orlando. The weather was perfect for travel too. With highs in the 90s, the weather forecast predicted a ten-percent chance of rain with minimal cloud cover.

The group agreed to meet up at the McDonalds near Fabian's house. Fabian's place was minutes from the Florida Turnpike, a major thoroughfare. It's one straight shot to Orlando with periodic tolls.

Everyone was psyched about the trip. Shanda couldn't stop checking in on social media, exposing the group's travel pattern. Her behavior annoyed Kim, who insisted on maintaining privacy. Bill was the group's organizer. For the past 15 years, he coordinated the travel plans and pressured trip-goers to purchase their entrance and express passes early. David and Matt were returning members to the group since they were Bill's fraternity brothers and had attended the initial Horror Nights trip 15 years earlier.

And then there was Ray, the rambunctious traveler who everyone acknowledged as the life of the party.

Ray walked up to Fabian's car with a McDonald's bag in tote. Fabian sat in the driver's seat while Bill planted himself in the "shot gun" seat. Shanda sat behind Bill. Everyone else was piled up into the other vehicle and ready to go.

"I'm horny," Ray admitted.

Everyone laughed.

"What else is new?" Bill asked. "You're horny on every trip."

"I hope I meet someone this time," Ray added.

"Well, I'm glad you got your own room this year," Shanda commented. "I'm not having any of that this year."

"Yep, and Fabian, once we get to Orlando, I'm gonna need to stop at a CVS," Ray requested.

"For some condoms?" Fabian asked.

"And other stuff. I need food!" Ray exclaimed. "Snacks for the night."

"How cute. You're being hospitality to your freaks," Bill said.

"Alright, Bill," Ray warned, giving Bill the eye.

"I'm just saying. You better be careful. Make sure you and your freaks wear raincoats," Bill said.

"We do," Ray said.

Ray pressed the access code on his phone and opened Grindr, a hookup app used to connect with other gay users in the area.

Two hours later, the caravan was well on its way to Orlando.

Ray kept the group entertained as disc jockey, playing songs from his iPhone's playlist. He also surfed Grindr. The app identified 24 users online in Port St. Lucie, the rest stop that the group would visit within ten minutes. One particular user's name was "Boriqua84," with a profile picture of a man with a hairless, chiseled chest. He was 6'1" and weighed 180 pounds. The profile also revealed his anatomical features and sexual preference, a top. Ray licked his lips.

For half an hour, the two flirted and exchanged private pics through the app.

Coincidentally, Boriqua84 was in route to Orlando too. He and his friends planned to stop at the Port St. Lucie rest stop.

"I gotta use the bathroom," Ray lied.

"We're stopping in a few," Fabian announced.

"That's not all you want to do in St Lucie. Who did you meet on that app?" Shanda asked.

She had been watching Ray.

Ray chuckled and said, "My future baby daddy."

At the rest stop, everyone dispersed to Burger King, Earl's Sandwiches, Starbucks, or the restroom. Bill got in line for an Earl's sandwich. Ray kept him company. Ray scanned the area for any trace of Boriqua84. The array of beautiful men enamored him.

And then he spotted Mr. Sunshine standing about 20 feet away.

Mr. Sunshine wore a yellow tank top and rainbow-colored shorts so high that they looked like swimwear. He spotted Ray and smiled. Ray smiled too.

"Shit," Ray thought. "He's fine as hell, but he's not Boriqua84… too short."

Suddenly, a young woman in her 20s grabbed Mr. Sunshine's arm. Ray rolled his eyes.

Bill nudged Ray and asked, "What are you looking at?"

"That," Ray said, motioning in Mr. Sunshine's direction.

"Oh, that," Bill said. "But he's got a girl."

"Straight, bi, gay, who cares?" Ray commented sarcastically.

"Until you get abducted and your face is spread across the 6 o'clock news. No dick is worth that, man," Bill said.

"Yeah, yeah…" Ray responded.

He checked the app once more. Boriqua84 was a few feet away.

Ray looked around, this time scanning the Burger King line.

He saw Mr. Technology standing in a moderately long line and looking at his phone. Two other unattractive males accompanied him. He was a tall Hispanic male and wore glasses. He wore a carbon colored t-shirt with the words "Built in the U.S.A." Ray thought he was gorgeous. He watched Mr. Technology press the keys on his phone.

Then a *ding* sounded on Ray's phone. Ray unlocked the phone and opened the app. Boriqua84 responded.

"Where are you?" Borqiua84 typed.

"In Port St. Lucie," Ray typed.

There was a pause. Mr. Technology typed busily on his phone and started looking around. Ray stood nearby, but he didn't make himself known just yet.

"Me too," Ray responded, looking in Mr. Technology's direction.

Mr. Technology turned around and spotted Ray. They stared at each another. Then they both smiled. Mr. Technology got out of line and walked over to Ray, who parted from Bill.

No words were spoken at first. Ray examined him. Mr. Technology appeared even taller up close. His slight beard stubble and glasses made him look like a sexy nerd. He had large hands and even larger feet.

Ray was in gay heaven.

"Wow," he said.

"Nice," Mr. Technology replied.

"What's your name?" Ray asked.

"Chris. Nice to meet you," Chris said, "And Yours?"

"I'm Ray."

They shook hands. Ray felt something in Chris' grip. His nice, warm hand was titillating. Ray wanted him badly.

"I'm staying at the Rosen Inn on International Drive. And you?" Ray inquired.

I'm staying at the La Quinta Inn close by," Chris said. "I'll message you my number."

"Alright, maybe we can hang out later," Ray said, smiling.

"Sounds good. Look. I gotta go. Hit me up, alright?" Chris asked with a smile.

Ray watched him walk away.

Later that evening, after everyone had arrived to Orlando and checked in, the group walked across International Drive to a local attraction, Fun Spot. From midway rides to arcade games, everyone could find something entertaining to do. Bill and Fabian challenged the group to a goat car race. Everyone but Ray, who stood aside, participated. The night air was calm and humid. As the bell rang to start the race, Ray pulled out his phone to text Chris.

"What u doing?" Ray texted.

"Waiting 4 u," Chris typed, seconds later.

"I'm in room 112 on the first floor. You can park outside my door if you find space. Can u get away?" Ray asked.

"I can. Text me when you're back in your room. I'll be there in 90 minutes, I guess," Chris responded.

"Okay."

Ray locked his phone and turned to cheer on his comrades, who at the moment were nearing the second bend of the racetrack.

"Ding" went the text message on his phone. Ray unlocked the phone to read the message. It was probably Chris.

"You finally in town?" The text stated.

Oh, shit, Ray thought. Ron, Ray's ex, lived in Orlando too. He and Ray still saw each other on occasion. Ray reminisced. Ron was 5' 11", 175 pounds and a musician. They dated for two years before deciding to part ways after trials of drama and unsettled circumstances. But they thrived better as friends, especially friends with benefits.

"I can't wait to see you. Tonight? I'm staying at the Rosen on International 6327," Ray typed.

"Text me when you're back in your room," Ron texted.

"Okay."

Ray asked Fabian to swing by the CVS on their way back to the hotel. Ray rushed inside to purchase his evening delights: a pint of Breyer's Vanilla Bean ice cream, a box of Trojan condoms, a gallon of Zephyrhills water, two banana-flavored moon pies, one honey bun, and a bag of ranch-flavored Doritos. When he returned to the car, Bill looked at Ray and shook his head in disappointment.

"Nobody should be on a diet when they're on vacation," Ray suggested.

Ray finally made it back to his hotel room.

He showered and laid across the bed, waiting for any text. Finally, it came. There was a light rap on the door. Through the peep hole, Ray could see Chris in the faint light.

Ray opened the door. Chris looked more scrumptious than ever. He wore sweatpants and a white tank top. Ray invited him in.

They made their way to the bed and sat down. Chris reached over and touched Ray's right thigh. Ray grabbed Chris' hand. The same fire they exchanged at the rest stop began to rekindle.

Then a *ding* sounded from Ray's phone.

"Shit, hold on," Ray said as he unlocked the phone to respond to the text. Chris, slightly annoyed, waited for Ray to finish.

"Can't it wait?" Chris asked.

Ray put the phone down. They proceeded to make out. Chris dined on Ray's thick lips. Chris' breath smelled like spearmint gum; the scent aroused Ray.

Then there was a knock at the door.

"Expecting someone?" Chris asked with a confused look on his face.

"Wait," Ray said.

He got up to open the door. Standing in the doorway was Ron, his ex.

Chris was dumbfounded. Ray was speechless. Both men did not anticipate a third member for the night.

"This is awkward, so let's get this out of the way. Chris, Ron, Ron, Chris," Ray proudly introduced.

The men refused to shake hands.

"It won't change things. You both can have me. Together or by yourself," Ray said confidently.

He smiled. Ron smiled back. Chris frowned.

Ray quickly searched for the "do not disturb" sign to hang on the doorknob, but he couldn't find one. So he went over to this suitcase and removed a large white tube sock.

He opened the door and tied the sock on the doorknob.

"Room service won't be waking me up in the morning," Ray thought.

He closed the door.

The next morning, Ray met his friends for breakfast. By the time he had arrived, Fabian and Bill had already finished their meals. Matt and David were in the buffet line piling their plates. Kim and Shanda chatted away about the night before.

Ray sat down at the table.

"Someone had a long night," Bill began.

"What do you mean?" Ray asked, smiling.

"You know what he means. We saw that sock hanging on your door," Shanda confessed.

Ray laughed. "And?"

"So you finally met that Boriqua87 guy?" Fabian inquired.

"Boriqua84," Ray corrected. "And his name is Chris."

Matt and David returned to the table with full breakfast plates.

"It was just hanging there," Shanda continued. "That sock."

"If that sock could talk. I wonder what would it say?" Bill added.

"Help me!" Shanda exclaimed. Everyone laughed.

"Don't your ass get tired?" Bill asked.

"I don't kiss and tell," Ray responded.

By midday, Ray received two simultaneous messages from Ron and Chris.

"I had a great time last night," Ron typed.

Ray replied with a smiling emoji.

"I never want to see you again," Chris texted.

Ray blocked his number.

Hooked Up on Tinder

*R*IHANA'S "WE FOUND Love" played in the background through a wireless speaker. The speaker was shaped like a pile of poop, a popular emoji. Warren couldn't help but laugh at himself.

He was searching for love in a hopeless place.

Warren held his iPhone in the palm of his left hand surfing the Tinder app. Beautiful and busted women's profiles montaged across his screen. He swiped left, eliminating a few of the ugly chicks. One profile, "Trixie10," caught his attention, and she was hot. She looked like a southern white girl with all the right finishes… dirty blonde hair draped nicely over her shoulder, crystal blue eyes that light up any day, and that gorgeous smile, the type that he wanted to wake up to in the morning. Warren swiped right on her profile.

Then he slid into her private, direct message.

"Hey, you're cute," he started.

At first she didn't respond. After two minutes, she answered.

"Hello, there. You're not so bad yourself," Trixie10 typed.

"I like your profile. What are you looking for tonight?" he asked.

"Good, quality company," she typed. "As long as you're okay with my girlfriend watching."

Warren paused.

He had been around the block, but he had never been with two chicks at the same time. There's a first for everything, he thought.

"That's fine," he continued, followed by a wink Emoji.

"Send me your number, baby," Trixie10 insisted.

And the conversation continued.

Ninety minutes later, they met up at a local Starbucks. As Warren entered, the smell of freshly brewed coffee waivered through the air. He surveyed the area, checking for a 5'3" woman wearing a turquoise shirt and designer jeans. Trixie10 sat at the table just to the right of him. She looked in his direction and smiled, waiving at him to join her.

She stood to greet him.

"Damn, you're fine, mami," he began, studying her from head to toe.

"You look good too. I didn't realize you were that tall," she replied.

He bent over and pecked her on the cheek.

"Can I get you something?" he offered.

"I'm good, thanks," she said. "I'm not much into coffee."

"But I'll take some…" another voice said. A woman approached Warren from behind.

A thicker, more solidly-built woman stepped forward. She wasn't as friendly as Trixie10.

"I didn't know you were inviting someone…" he responded jokingly while eyeing the butch woman.

"I gotta make sure you're the one. Not everyone can be with my girl, you know what I mean?" Butch-girl remarked.

"This is awkward," Warren said. "Look, have a seat. We should talk first."

He scooted his seat over to the right, closer to Trixie10 and making room for Butch-girl.

"Slow down, man," Butch-girl commanded. "Your place is over there."

She pointed to an open spot directly across from Trixie10 and her. Then she sat down next to her woman and pecked her on the cheek.

The contrast between the two women was so stark. Butch-girl was clearly the dominant in the relationship. At a quick glance, she looked like a short, chubby man with a Napoleon complex. She had a *low boy* haircut and wore a turquoise Nike t-shirt and sagging, black Nike sweatpants. From head to toe, she was a walking billboard for the local Nike Outlet.

"Bull-daggers always pull the finest bitches," Warren pondered.

He studied the odd couple.

"Tanya told me that she found you on Tinder," Butch-girl said. "So *this* is what you want, bae?"

"Yes, I do," Trixie10 replied.

"I thought I was meeting two lipstick lesbians," Warren said, smirking.

"Watch your mouth, man. Don't try me," Butch-girl warned.

"Look, I don't mean any harm. I just want to have a good time. You know?" he chided.

Tanya smiled while Butch-girl looked on in contempt.

"So what you into?" Butch-girl asked.

"Anything… could be both of you at the same time if you're down. You clean?" he asked.

"Yes, we are both negative. We stay tested. We hope you are too," Butch-girl said.

"I am. So… I guess I'll do your girl while you…"

"Who said you're doing her?" Butch-girl asked.

Warren's eyes widened.

"Meaning?" he asked.

"Meaning, you ain't here for her… you're here for me," Butch-girl retorted.

Warren was speechless. A knot formed in his throat. Butch-girl was unattractive in every possible way. Even under the strongest drug or most exciting porn, there was no way that he'd stay hard for such an ugly bitch.

"How much you offering?" he asked.

"Well, Trixie10 said your going rate is $100 per hour with extra for anything else. That's what it said in his profile, bae, right?" Butch-girl asked.

Tanya nodded.

"And I'm going to need a whole lot of liquor," Warred added, examining the two women. He winked at Tanya.

"I'll join once you two get started. That's the agreement we discussed," Tanya added. "Besides, bi-guys are supposed to be the most understanding, you know, in situations like this. At least that's what you said."

Warren mentally cringed. His words had come back to kick him in the ass. "Karma is a big, fat bitch with no batteries in her vibrator," he thought.

The drive to Biscayne Boulevard was a short one. The Miami humidity seized him as he exited his parked car, a pearl-colored Tesla. The couple was spending the weekend at the Vagabond Hotel. In the recent years, the hotel had been renovated and restored to its proper use and function. In the 1950s, it was a booming location for vacationing celebrities and other travelers who wanted to stay in the pulse of Miami, a then evolving city. Now the hotel was a mid-century modern for the in-crowd. One weekend each month was gay night. House music thumped in the air. Barely-clothed bodies adorned the poolside. The bar was located just a few feet away, where bottles and drinks were traveling in every direction. Though predominately male, the scene had its few shares of lesbians and gay-hags alike sprinkled throughout the place. Good vibes lingered.

Warren passed a gay couple chatting on the second landing of the hotel. One guy was smoking an e-cigarette. They both looked at Warren as he walked by and smiled.

"If only I were banging those two tonight… instead I got Godzilla waiting for me…" he thought.

He rapped on the door of the hotel room. No one answered. He knocked again, but there was still no reply. Puzzled, he pulled out his phone from his pocket to message Tanya. Just as he unlocked his phone the door opened…

Tanya stood there wearing a two-piece bikini bathing suit and flip-flops. Warren's jaw dropped. She was a tasty tease to him but an obedient submissive to the Butch-girl beast.

"I'm going to the pool," she said as she walked past Warren.

He watched her walk toward the two guys he passed on his way to the room. He stood there in the doorway and he felt even more confused by the circumstance.

He entered the room.

The room was dark with a small lamp lit to the far left of the bed. There was no sign of Butch-girl anywhere. Sounds could be heard coming from the nearby bathroom. He closed the door behind him. He remained still as he watched the light under the bathroom door go. The door opened.

Butch-girl came out wearing a tank top, basketball shorts, and locker room Adidas slides. From the dim light he could see that she was indeed a woman with moderately developed tits. Warren noticed how well she filled out compared to her girlfriend. She walked past him and sat at the foot of the Queen-sized bed. As she passed him, he caught a scent, a mix of baby powder and Cognac.

Because this was work, Warren needed to be as professional as possible. He slowly walked over to the bed and sat adjacent to Butch-girl with his back toward her. He glanced over his shoulder at her. She looked over at him and smiled. He patted the spot next time him, inviting her to join him.

They sat in the silence of the room, facing the unpowered flat screen television.

She could feel the heat cascade off of him. Delicately, she placed her right hand adjacent to his left hand while still looking forward. His pinky finger moved over to greet her own. The touch was electrifying. She couldn't resist his advances. Her sensual instincts kicked in, stirring up dormant desires.

He moved in to her face, gently touching it with his left hand. He brought her face to his and focused on her enticing lips...

"I can't, man. I'm sorry," she said as she pulled away from him.

She stood up. Her back faced him.

"We could just talk," he recommended.

"About what?"

"You. Me. How the hell did we get here, anyway?" He questioned.

They laughed.

For the next hour, they shared their life stories. Warren was originally born in Guyana but later arrived in the states at age ten. His mother was an elementary school teacher and his father was unknown. As he grew older, he had begun to come to terms with what he wanted most: to be everything and anything his father was not to him.

Butch-girl revealed her true name... Maggie.

Maggie was a tomboy who'd grown up in the Hialeah, Florida, with two biological parents, a dog, a kid brother and an *abuelita*. Around middle school, she realized she was much more attracted to girls than guys and began getting into fights with the prissy girls who did not like her back. The boys were intimidated yet fascinated with her nature while some girls saw her as another cool chick, just one they would never undress in front of. By twenty-one, Maggie had had three run-ins with the law, one leading to a Florida charge for drug trafficking. Eventually, she met Tanya and they became friends and later lovers.

For another three hours, they sat at the foot of the bed, sharing life's journeys and misfortunes. The more Maggie spoke, the more Warren realized that she was just like every other chick, one longing for companionship and understanding. Her tough exterior softened by the hour. Butch-girl wasn't half bad after all.

By 2 a.m., the door opened, and Tanya returned half drunk and half excited about something. She found Warren and Maggie propped up in bed, naked, and smiling.

"Well, I guess it all worked out, huh?" Tanya joked.

She walked to the bathroom and shut the door.

Warren and Maggie looked at each other and burst into laughter.

"Should we tell her the truth?" Warren asked.

"Nah," Maggie responded. "But your idea worked."

They fist-pumped one another. Warren slowly climbed out of bed, wearing his underwear.

"I must admit," he continued as he dressed, "You're the first woman I've ever been to bed with and never banged."

"There's a first for everything," she joked as she watched him dress. "The talk was better than any lay I've had. Thanks, man."

Leeches

LEECHES… THEY COULD suck the blood from any open wound. Weird species, they could be. I could admit that every leech has its value, it's purpose…

Except the one that was sitting across from me.

I let my brother Evan choose the location, Cheesecake Factory at the Dadeland Mall, since it was his birthday. When we arrived to the restaurant, the hostess greeted me and logged my name in her queue. Then she gave me a transponder to alert me when my table was ready. The wait was forty-five minutes.

The leech and I stood there, waiting.

I loved my brother. As knuckle-headed as he could be, I had nothing but love for him. We had been through so much together. Despite the arguments, we remained a family. Our bond remained stronger and more durable than ever. Even though we were different men, we valued each other, including our choices of women, our faiths, our friends…

Except one friend, Larry the leech.

I was disinterested in engaging him. Instead I people watched to pass the time, occasionally checking my phone for a text or social media alert. He entertained himself with his phone. I couldn't see what he was up to. I was grateful for the silence between us. Being fake would make me sick.

"But it was Evan's birthday," I kept telling myself.

I didn't protest his wish to invite Larry. Evan was a lot closer to Larry than I, and I didn't understand their friendship.

Larry was a bonafide liar.

The man lied so badly that if he said it was raining, I'd have to look outside the window to check. His lies were about the most ridiculous, asinine things too. No one gave a crap if was buying a new iPhone or that his boss would gift him bottles of Black Label. I preferred friends who lived in reality and with their feet planted on the ground. After two years of knowing Larry, I had come to realize he needed material items or people's statuses to validate his existence.

Well, those were his life choices. Yes, I judged him. I couldn't stand it anymore to have him around me.

An hour later, we were seated at the table and still no sign of Evan. I pulled out my iPhone to text him.

"Where you at, man?" I texted.

About two minutes later came the reply.

"Parking now. See you soon."

When Evan arrived, he made the grand entrance he was always known for. His navy blue New York Yankees' hat complimented his ivory colored button down. With skinny jeans and a pair of white Yeezys, my brother enjoyed sporting labels. He walked up to the table and Larry stood, welcoming Evan with a brotherly hug. I did the same.

Thank goodness Evan was there. I grew tired of staring at Larry's ugly mug.

Evan and Larry caught up with each other. They chatted about sports and kids. Eventually, Evan complimented his watch. Larry said it was another gift from his boss. I cringed.

By the time the main entrée arrived, I felt sick to my stomach… and it was not because of the food. Listening to Larry gloat about his next travel pursuits or the women he had banged was nauseating. I tried to maintain my cool, yet Evan was content with it all. Occasionally, Evan would glance over at me to check if I was okay. I faked a smile. I knew that in another hour or so, the madness would be over.

Minutes later, Evan left for the restroom, leaving Larry and me to interact without him.

The waitress walked over to check on us. Cute girl, about 23 with a huge butt. Larry was mesmerized. He glanced over at me after she passed.

"So you'd hit that?" He asked.

"Nah, not my type," I answered. "I'm a happily married man."

"And how's that working for you?" He inquired.

"The same way it's working for you… oh, wait. You're not married. Guess those lonely winter nights make porn that much more inviting, huh?" I chided.

Larry didn't find my joking funny.

"Why do we have beef, man? It's been over two years and we still don't click. Why?" Larry asked.

"I'll tolerate you the moment you stop faking who you really are," I said.

"So that's it? You hate me because you really don't know me?"

"I don't hate, man. I dislike people who aren't genuine. The moment you introduce that man to me, we'll be cool," I responded.

I had had enough. Each hair on my arms stood as I raised my tone. Each syllable I uttered brought back the constant reminder that Larry is just another idiot I didn't want to engage with.

Evan returned and dinner was over. Dessert followed with the traditional waitress staff singing "happy birthday" to my brother as onlookers watched and sang along. Our waitress cutie returned to deliver the bill.

A week prior, I begrudgingly texted Larry to tell him that we'd split the bill evenly in honor of my brother's birthday.

So I reached for my wallet; however, Larry just sat there. I grew outraged.

"Uh, damn, man. I left my wallet at home," he acknowledged.

I had officially had it. The room grew dark and I could hardly see. I blacked out when I was angry. It took a few minutes for me to make it out.

After regaining myself, I opened my wallet and threw my credit card on the table.

"And why am I not surprised?!" I yelled.

The couple at the neighboring table looked over at us, but I didn't care.

"Man, I'll spot you. You got Cash app? I'll send you the difference through the app," Larry offered, trying to sound sincere.

"I can get it, it's no big deal, man," my brother offered.

"Hell no, it's your birthday. I don't mind treating YOU," I said.

Moments later, the tab was settled and my brother said his farewells to Larry after they made promises to meet up the following weekend at a dive bar. I was invited, but I declined. Larry held out his hand to thank me; I refused to touch him. I was thrilled to watch him walk away from us in search of his car.

"I don't like leeches," I commented to my brother as Larry walked away. Evan started laughing.

"But every leech has a purpose," he said.

Puzzled, I looked at him. My brother had a wide grin.

"He still doesn't know I'm banging his ex," he said slyly.

I didn't know if I should have been pissed off or proud of my brother in that moment. But for some reason, vindication felt so damn good.

The leech had enjoyed his last good meal… at my expense.

Marital Secrets

"YOU SURE you wanna move there? I mean, there are so many blacks there," Lina questioned with an earnest look on her face.

"Last time I checked, I was black too," Clyde responded.

For years, his sister and he could really never see eye to eye. Petty childhood arguments led to bitter sibling warfare their parents couldn't mend. Aging was supposed to mature people... well, most people at least. Maturity skipped out on their relationship.

Clyde's choice to move to North Miami was based on several factors. For one, the Miami commute during rush-hour traffic could not be any worse since he took the job at the new firm in downtown Ft. Lauderdale. South Florida is just too crowded, he thought. Sunshine dollars were costly.

Lina stared at him. He saw her dark brown eyes revealing the doubt of his decision. She knew him well even if he didn't want to admit it. But Clyde didn't like anyone telling him how to spend his money.

"And what does Barbara think?" Lina inquired.

"She's fine as long as I'm happy," he replied.

"Dumb girl," Linda retorted.

"Know what's so sad?"

"What?" she asked.

"You're unhappy. And as long as you're unhappy, you don't want anyone else around you to be happy. That's why you don't have shit."

"Fuck you!" Lina exclaimed.

"I gotta go," he said.

Minutes later, he was in his car driving away from his sister's place.

The same scene played out between them again and again; the scene always ended the same too. One sibling pounced on the other and the other one walking away in agony.

"If wish we could choose our families like we can choose our friends," he thought.

When he arrived home, the house was dark. Daylight disappeared at 6 p.m., typical December winters in Florida. The emptiness embraced Clyde. The blinds were still open too; one street light lit up the place.

He surveyed the living room while standing in the dark. Things were undisturbed. The house seemed to miss the shouting, slamming doors, and fake apologies.

But not Clyde.

The signs told him that Lina must be working late again for the fifth night in a row and the kids were staying at her mother's house for the night. For a week, the couple had barely spoken to one another since their verbal showdown in the kitchen...

Clyde was standing by the coffee maker, sipping his usual cup of decaffeinated coffee. Lina stood behind him, ranting about how the pool or lawn needing maintenance of some sort.

The more she complained, the more he sipped. The taste of decaffeinated blend was pleasing, Not too much sugar and easy on the creamer. His tongue stung a bit from coffee, but he liked it that way. The pain he endured for coffee was far better than the pain he invested in marriage. In a flash, Lina grabbed a full cup of coffee and hurled it at Clyde. He ducked, causing glass to splatter everywhere across the kitchen counter and floor. She kneeled down and sobbed. In just three years, their marriage was destined for closure.

He continued to drink his coffee, staring at Barbara. Her frizzy, curly hair made her look like an estranged woman. Her tired, red eyes told the truth. They spoke of frustration. Clyde tried to conjure positive images of the woman he had fallen in love with years ago, but those images were tarnished by anger.

Barbara stared at her husband.

"How did we get here, Clyde?" She asked with a concerned look.

Slowly, he replied, "I honestly don't know."

"Do you still love me?" She asked.

"I do… but I love me more."

"What the hell is that supposed to mean?" She inquired.

"It means what it means. I'm willing to work on us but I have to work on me."

"Then come with me to counseling," she pleaded. "We can work through this."

She wiped a teardrop from her right cheek. To her left was a picture on the kitchen counter of her, him and the kids. The pretty picture frame was titled "memories."

"I want that again," she said, pointing at the picture. Her left hand trembled.

He continued to sip coffee. Only a small amount remained. His life and coffee were one in the same in that moment, both running out of time or abundance; and he didn't want any refills.

Minutes later, he was back in his car, backing out of the driveway. As he turned forward, he caught a glimpse of his wife standing at the doorway. Her figure blended with the darkness and the house as he drove away. He drove leaving pain and frustration behind him.

Blue Martini had to be better.

The bar was nestled in the heart of Kendall, Florida, the suburbs. For the 40 and up crowd, it was a great place to relax and vibe, even solo. For a Friday night, anything was better than arguing. Valet parking was $20. He searched his wallet, but only found a ten. So he sharked for a parking space in the overcrowded, free lot.

After parking, he checked himself in the driver's visor mirror. For the day he had had, he looked remarkable fresh. Jet-black hair was styled and teased with mousse. His oily face still beamed with possibility. He heard the car door slam close next to his car. An older man and younger woman exited the vehicle and embraced as they walked toward the bar. Clyde took one last glance and smiled at himself in the mirror.

The night didn't have to be so bad after all.

As expected, Blue Martini was packed with patrons. Clyde was lucky to grab the last available barstool. He ordered a Jack Daniel on the rocks. Walter, the bartender, smiled and gave Clyde the drink.

"One of those days?" Walter questioned.

Clyde gulped the drink down quickly. He savored the flavor. It had ended too quickly.

"You can say that," Clyde responded, downing the last ounce of liquor in the glass.

"Second Jack Daniel coming up," Walter said as he worked to replenish Clyde's glass.

Clyde scanned the room. The bar was filled with all types of people. A group of women toasted a lady wearing a "Bride to Be" sash. Two men sat chatting away near the women. One woman was sitting closest to Clyde, waiting for someone. She looked in his direction and then immediately looked away.

Walter noticed Clyde staring at the woman.

"Brother, you don't want any of that," he warned as he slid the liquor-filled glass over to Clyde.

"You're right, that's not what I'm looking for," he assured as he drank.

"What are you looking for?" Walter asked.

"What time do you get off?"

Then Walter intermittently talked about his life after leaving Argentina with his family as he served bar patrons. He was five when he left and had no clue of what was happening. His father promised that life would be different in Miami where more family was living the good life in Coral Gables. Walter's uncle was a banker and worked for years dealing in international trade markets. The family arrived with nothing but a few suitcases of their belongings and empty promises of support from family and friends in America.

What they got when they arrived was a nightmare.

The uncle was suddenly arrested for racketeering, causing the Feds to seize all of his valuable assets. Eventually, the family had to seek refuge elsewhere. Walter's mother had a friend who lived in South Dade down in the Cutler Bay area. The older Cuban woman lived alone with three cats, two dogs, and a nosy homeowner's association.

The more Walter talked, the less Clyde cared to listen. Another typical immigrant sob story, he thought. But Walter was being genuine. When it was time to pay the tab, Clyde discovered that his drinks were discounted. In appreciation, he offered Walter a ride home.

As he drove, Clyde's stomach started to grumble. He pulled into a nearby Wendy's.

"Want something from Wendy's?" he offered Walter.

"I'll take a number two with medium fries and Coke," Walter responded, grabbing for his wallet.

"My treat, man. You've been nice to me tonight. The least I can do is feed you."

Clyde smiled.

"Alright. I appreciate it, man," Walter thanked.

When they arrived at Walter's, the complex's lot was full. For a couple of minutes, Clyde searched and finally found a vacant parking space. As they walked to Walter's building, Clyde stopped in his tracks.

"Hear that?"

"What?" Walter asked, looking around.

"That's the thing. I hear nothing. And it's nice."

Walter smiled. "Yeah, I guess."

Both men were hungry. Three cheeseburgers, French fries, and vanilla frosties were sprawled across the table. Walter sniffed a fry and then popped it into his mouth. Clyde laughed. Then Walter turned on Pandora to his favorite playlist. Adele's voice boomed through the wireless speakers.

"You can't listen to her when you're heading to work," Clyde advised.

"You telling me. Adele will make your day lousy," Walter added.

"Especially if you already feel like shit."

"Eat, man. The food's getting cold."

Later, they are sitting on Walter's futon, which was adjacent from the flat-screen Sony. Walter offered Clyde a beer before taking a spot on the futon next to Clyde.

The studio apartment smelled pleasant due to a vanilla bean Glade plug-in. Walter was unusually tidy for a guy too. The kitchen looked spotless. In fact, Clyde wondered if the man even knew how to use it since it was so well kept. Ikea Billy shelves stood on each side of the television. Adjacent to the futon was an older, burgundy chair. Two stools adorned the mini-counter facing the kitchen. The door to the bedroom was wide open. A small lamp on a nightstand illuminated the bedroom. Walter had a sense of taste and style.

The apartment was the antithesis of Clyde's house. With the beer bottle still in his hand, he closed his eyes for a brief moment. He tried to listen for it, the sounds of the slamming doors and half apologies. But they never came.

"Thanks for the ride home and for dinner," Walter said.

"No problem, man." Clyde's eyes remained closed.

"Next time it's on me," Walter offered.

"Of course."

The Pandora song changed. Usher's voice crooned through the speakers. Clyde began to move his head to the rhythm. His waist began to gyrate slightly in a circular motion. He put his drink down and stood up. The scene changed.

He was no longer in Walter's apartment but transferred to a stage in a big amphitheater. People and lights were everywhere. People shouted Clyde's name over and over. He walked to the center of the stage and grabbed the mic from the microphone stand. He braced for the first note when…

"Man, you okay?" Walter inquired.

"Sorry, I got lost," Clyde replied.

The performance was just a figment of his imagination.

"Okay, good. Thought you were gone, man. And I didn't spike your drink," Walter joked.

He placed his hand on the futon, close to Clyde's.

Something stirred inside Clyde. It wasn't a bad feeling, just different. This apartment made him feel some kind of way. He struggled to fight his emotions.

"This is weird," Clyde admitted.

"Yeah, I agree. When are you going to tell her?"

Clyde opened his eyes and looked at Walter, confused.

"What do you mean, tell her? About what?" Clyde asked.

"You know exactly what I'm talking about. When are you going to tell her?" Walter's relentlessness started to kill the mood.

"When I'm good and ready…" was all Clyde could say.

Walter reached over and grabbed Clyde's hand. Clyde responded, gripping Walter's. Walter reached over and grabbed the remote control. He started surfing Netflix's menu.

For the rest of the evening, they got lost in the symphonies of pop culture and the realism of marital secrets.

Truth Be Told

SO IT'S BEEN said that when "life gives you lemons, make lemonade." Well, I don't like lemons and hate lemonade even more. I prefer my drinks a bit sour, actually. It's the taste you don't want to remember anytime soon.

I don't hate men... I hate women. They suck. One minute they mess with your heart and the next they leave you for another dude... or chick... or whatever. Giving your all to a cause has its consequences...

And then the writing stopped.

Belkys put down her pen and journal and stared out her bedroom window. In the distance she could see a purple and gold hue cascade the land as the sun set. Another day was gone... another battle also won, and the declared winner? Writer's block.

Getting ready for work was the same-old routine. She took a long, hot shower, hoping that the moment would never end. She tied her hair up into a bonnet for uniform purposes. Her makeup was minimal. Her uniforms was the same soot- colored slacks to match an even drearier shirt.

Belkys was ready for another day in the food service industry.

The Uber arrived as promised within seven minutes. It took fourteen steps to make it from the apartment doorway to the car. Twenty-eight minutes later, she arrived at Applebee's. Fifty-six minutes later, Belkys encountered her first hot-tempered patron, one who promised no tip and to report her to management.

"Alright, then," Belkys responded.

With her head hung low, she walked away from the table.

To appease the patron, her manager promised him a free dessert and a discount on the bill. The table's speaker, a lanky, mocha-complexioned fellow, shook his head as he watched Belkys be reassigned to another area away from his party's table.

Belkys wasn't the problem. It was his jerk of a friend who thought it was okay to bequeath his frustrations on her.

"Let's go," Chris said to his friends. "It's time to go."

As he walked out of the restaurant, he passed Belkys' area. Her back was to him. If only he had the nerve to apologize on behalf of his friend for making her night a near-fuck up. Moments later, he was standing outside of the restaurant's entrance. The night air was calm and inviting. Definitely, the night was still young. He parted his friends and walked toward his car.

At 3:05 a.m., the Lyft arrived to pick Belkys up after her late shift. She toted the meal she could not chump down during break time in a white Applebee's take-out bag as well as her purse. She entered the car, a four-door Toyota Camry. French vanilla aromas waivered in the air. One thing she hated more than lemons was the smell of Vanilla…. of any kind.

"Hello," the driver greeted her, peering at her directly through the rearview mirror.

"Hi," Belkys greeted in a tired voice.

Taylor Swift's, "Shake It Off" played lowly through the stereo speakers. The driver moved his head to the rhythm of the song. He kept his eyes on the road.

"I'm Chris," he began.

"Hi, Chris," she replied. She wasn't in the mood for small talk.

"Do you always work late shifts?" He asked.

"That's none of your business," she retorted.

"Sorry. I didn't mean to offend you," he apologized.

Swift's lyrics began to play in her head, "Shake it off, shake it off..." If only she could. For years, Belkys built a wall around her heart after the estranged breakup with her boyfriend of six years. Things were going well until they decided to relocate to another city and time... Miami. As foreigners to the city, they thought it would be best to live among the in-crowd of the Design District, which was an epic fail. New friends, new culture, and new languages. They were overwhelming and tested the couple's relationship. Next came the lay-offs and then the extended work shifts. Relocating to an apartment in Little Havanh didn't help much either.

The infidelity arrived, demolishing what was left of her relationship. Hurt and disappointed, Belkys packed her bags and headed to a friend's place. Life couldn't get any worse. She was stuck in a foreign city with ties to very few people. She felt like a fish out of water. *Shaking it off* wasn't that easy.

One year later, she was riding coach in a Lyft and working a dead-beat job that she hated. Life had a field day with Belky's heart, so much that perhaps it may be beyond repair. She stared out of the backseat window, watching as the car sped by streetlights and dimly lit homes where happy people probably slept. They all had more normal lives than she. They could go to bed at a reasonable hour and could have breakfast before heading out to careers or jobs they enjoyed.

Everyone feasted on success and happiness. Belkys could only imagine their tastes.

"So how did you end up with a gig like this?" She asked.

Chris looked at her face in the rearview mirror. Even though it was dark, he could still make out the distinct outline of its features. His eyes returned to the road.

"I lost my job at the courthouse and needed to make ends meet...
I didn't mean to offend you earlier."

"It's okay. I accept," she replied. "Sometimes I can be a bit of a
bitch to people when I'm pissed off."

"Why are you angry?" he questioned, glancing at her in the
mirror.

"Life sucks," she answered.

Chris lowered the volume of the stereo's volume.

"You can turn that off if you want to talk to me," Belkys suggested.
He turned the radio off.

For the next two minutes, silence enveloped the car's cabin. The
faint sounds of the car's engine. Belkys checked the arrival time on
her mobile app. Another twelve minutes and she would be home.

"My name is Belkys. It's nice to meet you."

Chris smiled.

"Nice to meet you, Belkys. But I already knew your name."

"How?" She asked in surprise.

"From your profile."

They both laughed. The laughter lifted the tension in the air.

For another five minutes, they each provided the other with
a sugarcoated overview of their life stories. Each one listened and
asked questions when appropriate. By the time they arrived to Belkys'
apartment complex, the mood was pleasant. Chris brought the car
to a stop at her building's walkway. Chris turned toward her as she
gathered her belongings from the backseat.

"Truth be told, Belkys. You're pretty cool."

"You are too, Chris. Thanks for *lyfting* my spirits, man."

He chuckled. *He got it,* she thought.

Their eyes met. Even in the dark, she could tell that there was
something special behind his. She imagined them dark brown or
hazel. His chiseled facial features made him appear much older.
He could be the ideal package. He got out the car. Then they were
standing face-to-face.

Her beauty enraptured him. She stood four inches shorter than
he. Her hair, once tied up in a bonnet, now hung loosely about her

neck in a wild yet mesmerizing sort of way. A slight, balmy wind teased her hair, making it more enticing.

She held out her hand to shake his. The moment she touched him, she felt a spark, something pure and original.

Belkys saw the beginning of a beautiful friendship.

"I felt bad for you when my friend was being such an asshole..." he said.

"It's okay. I've had worse," she replied.

Years later, they recount the moment they first met: Belkys, a heartbroken maiden, and Chris, the soul seeker. They were imperfect yet a fit for one another... Two kindred spirits lost in their respective places and times suddenly finding one another within the anguish of life's glaring headlights... or headlines. Two paths were meant to cross, intermingle, and co-exist... truth be told.

Roxanne

$\mathcal{M}$ONDAY MORNINGS WERE all the same. Ana woke to a crying four-month-old grandson, Terry. The baby was hungry. *Babies are people too, they just can't speak*, Ana thought.

Life in Cutler Bay, Florida, was classic suburbia. The peaceful community was comprised of middle-class families. One and two-story houses stood decadently on manicured lawns monitored by a homeowner's association. A man-made lake was near the security booth with a fountain spouting water in various directions. Ana's community was great for raising kids or retirement.

But Ana's living wasn't always so easy. Just a year ago, she buried her husband.

The transition was difficult. After the funeral, the insurance company informed her that her husband's policy had lapsed, resulting in no funds for the service. Ana borrowed from family members and close friends to pay the $8K bill. Her kids convinced her to retire from her nursing career although she still had three years left before retirement.

Life had changed.

She went from changing elderly patients' diapers to changing her grandson's diaper. She had gained ten extra pounds as well. But she didn't mind. She wouldn't have it any other way.

Terry recognized Ana as she approached his crib. His wide, dark-brown eyes stared back at her as she picked him and sniffed his bottom end. The baby laughed, thinking it was playtime. He needed changing. She grabbed a diaper and baby wipes, took Terry to the nearby bed, and laid him on it. He smiled. Ana smiled back.

Ana convinced her children to let her babysit the grandkids since it gave her something to do. She didn't want someone else babysitting her grandchildren. Terry's older brother, Emmanuel, had already started pre-K. Denise, Ana's daughter, was the mother of the two boys. Denise was a good daughter, helping Ana financially, spiritually, and emotionally.

Ana and the clean baby moved to the living room where she was watching her favorite show, *Real Housewives of Atlanta*. Her recent episode was on pause. She froze right on the scene where Nene was about to go off on Kenya. Ana pushed play and the show continued.

Terry stared back at her as he fed from the bottle. After his feeding, Ana hoped he'd go back to sleep so that he she could finish her show and a few errands.

Minutes later, the house phone rang.

"Shit," Ana thought. "Another distraction." She picked up the phone.

"Mrs. Simmons?" The lady's voice asked.

"Yes, who's this?" Ana asked.

"This is Wells Fargo and we're calling to invite you to apply for our new platinum…"

"No, thank you," Ana interrupted and immediately hung up the phone.

The episode continued. Nene walked out of the restaurant with Kenya in tow. *This is getting good*, Ana thought. Ana fancied in the glamour and glitz of the socialite lives of Atlanta's elite. She herself was born there, not too far from Peachtree Street. Her mother brought her and her siblings to Miami when Ana was ten. The new city wasn't so welcoming in those days. Her mother was single and uneducated; she couldn't find immediate work. Ana was grateful for her mother's decision. It brought her family to a better life.

Terry finished the bottle. Ana placed him over her right shoulder and started patting his back. Before the tenth pat, a loud belch bellowed from the baby. Ana laughed. Terry was full and well fed. In no time, he'd be sleeping again. She rocked him back and forth for a few minutes. He was at peace and cooing slightly.

Ding.

Now what? Ana picked up her iPhone and read the preview screen. "Ma, did you get my first text?" Shana inquired.

Ana punched the keys to reply. "Leave me along. I'm watching my show."

Seconds later, Shana replied, "Turn that crap off."

Ana replied, "Go back to work!"

"LOL, alright ma. Love u."

Thirty minutes later, the episode ended. Terry was asleep on the couch beside Ana. The house was calm and quiet. She looked right to stare out the window to the backyard. It was a beautiful day. From her angle, she could see the mango tree limbs swaying in the breeze. Buds were starting to grow. In a couple of months, mangoes would fall and be ready for the picking. The clothesline was just to the left of the tree. Ana's favorite lounge dress was the only thing hanging on the line. She remembered that she needed to wash and dry more clothing before the spring rain moved in. Miami weather could be very unpredictable in spring. One day it could be cold, and then the next day it could be hot as hell. But nothing beat the smell of line-dried clothes. They smelled like nature and Tide detergent; line-drying spared the light bill too.

Before starting her next episode of *Housewives*, she needed to gather the clothes from the washer. Terry slept peacefully and would probably do so for another hour.

Both the house phone and cellphone were on silent mode. No more disturbances. Ana was alone, finally, to do what she needed to do.

She hurried to the laundry room and grabbed a white laundry basket. She started dumping clothing into it. As she moved, somewhat hastily, she paused for a moment. She listened intently. *He's still sleeping*, she thought. She continued working.

The laundry room was located on the opposite side of the house from her master bedroom. The featured three bedrooms; each was immaculate in design detail. One was a guest bedroom while Lisa, Ana's second daughter, occupied the second room. Lisa's door was closed. She had left early that morning for class. At age twenty-four, she was a late bloomer but highly responsible. She contributed often to the household. Her full-time job not only helped her mother from time to time, but it also paid for her to have a leased five-series BMW. As long as she was enrolled in college, Ana didn't mind her staying there.

Ana walked past the bedroom door. *Silence. Good*, she thought. She kept walking.

As she passed the couch, she peered over to look at Terry, who slept soundly. It wasn't good to leave a baby unattended, especially on a couch where he could fall and hurt himself. But she needed to get those clothes on the line. Five minutes wouldn't matter. Ana hurried out the back door.

Grabbing the clothing pins, she set to work hanging each garment: another lounge dress with extra pink flowers, two bras, two t-shirts, and a pair of men's underwear. The menswear belonged to her nephew who had spent the night the week before. She hurried to hang the remaining garments.

Finally, she was back indoors. She returned to the couch and grabbed the remote control.

Just as she was about to hit the play button, she heard a sound. She glanced over at Terry who had shifted slightly but still remained asleep. At first, she sat there still and waiting for the sound, hoping it wouldn't repeat itself.

Then she heard it again. Ana knew every settling noise her house could make. The sound came from the guest side of the house.

Annoyed, she went to investigate.

She checked the laundry room and to see if something had fallen from a shelf. But everything was fine. What could that sound be?

Maybe it's the house settling, she thought. The wind was extra breezy outdoors.

She headed toward the guest bedroom but found… nothing.

The natural lighting engulfed the room making the it look very inviting. She thought of retiring there later for a nap with the baby.

Ana walked past the door to Lisa's room. Then she heard another sound.

She froze. For hours, she thought that she and Terry were the only ones in the house. Lisa wouldn't be back until late afternoon. She stared at the closed door.

Then she put her ear to the door and listened… nothing.

She waited a few more seconds. No other sound was heard. Ana turned to head back to the family room.

Then the sound came again.

This time, it was more pronounced than before. She put her ear back to the door. It sounded like something was hitting against the wall very gently. Lisa liked to sleep with the ceiling fan on while the A/C blasted a good 70 degrees Fahrenheit. Ana disliked her daughter's inability to turn unneeded power off.

But the sound came again. Something was moving inside Lisa's room.

Ana was gripped with fear.

She believed in ghosts and the spirit world. She didn't like Ouija boards and watching scary movies. In fact, she hated Halloween. Her views had nothing to do with religion but everything to do with superstition. *Meddling with the dead could be dangerous,* she thought. It didn't help that her daughters enjoyed pranking her; they got her good a few times when she had least expected it.

Now was not the time to play games, especially with a sleeping baby on the couch. But curiosity prevailed over fear. Turning the doorknob slowly, she pushed open the door just enough to peer inside.

She peaked through the slant in the opening. The window was closed. She tried to peer upward. The ceiling fan was turning slowly. She looked at the bed.

Someone was in bed...

Ana was scared beyond belief. She thought of her escape plan... to grab Terry and run like hell out the front door and next door to her neighbor's house.

Whoever was lying in that bed began to move. Sounds came from the bed. A pair of big black feet appeared from under the sheets. They were long, ugly, and masculine.

Ana's eyes widened.

She peered further into the room. Fear was gone yet her anger grew. Another set of feet came from under the sheets... a woman's, perfectly painted and recently-pedicured.

Two people were in bed having sex.

The female legs disappeared then legs appeared on top of the sheets. Both legs crossed over the man as she mounted up. More sighs and groans echoed from the room. Sounds of ecstasy came from the covers.

Ana was furious.

She ran to her hallway closet and grabbed the only thing she could thing of.

It was long, a former mop stick and hard. Green paint lacquer peeled near the handle end. It was her choice of weapons. Her children and grandkids had a name for that stick...

They called it *Roxanne*.

She went back to the door and pushed it wide open with Roxane in her right hand.

"Oh, hell naw, not in my house!" Ana exclaimed.

Lisa and her boyfriend stopped. Scared and naked, they stared at Ana, who held Roxanne firmly in her right hand.

"What the fuck is this?!" Ana shouted. "In my house?!"

"Mama, no," Lisa begged.

But it was too late.

Ana started swinging Roxanne in the air like she was beating a candy-stuffed piñata. Lisa grabbed the sheet and tried to cover herself. The man jumped immediately out of bed, naked and semi-erect.

"Ms. Simmons, I'm sorry," he apologized.

But it was too late.

Ana smacked him on his right leg near his scrotum. He yelped, trying to protect himself. But Ana was relentless in her attack. If people wanted to have sex, they needed to do it anywhere BUT inside her home.

Lisa begged her mother to stop hitting her boyfriend. But Ana kept hitting and hitting. The man jumped around and tried to grab his underwear off the floor.

"Get the fuck out of my house!" Ana yelled as she smacked him on the ass and back. She was a good hitter too, landing licks all over his body.

The young man retreated, but Ana followed suit. The action moved outside the bedroom and into the hallway. He ran for the front door. Terry woke up from the commotion and started crying.

But Ana didn't stop. She followed the young man.

And Lisa followed them. She had managed to put on a t-shirt and shorts. She picked up the crying baby from the couch.

Ana and boyfriend were now on the porch. And brandished Roxanne like a sword. The butt-naked man broke into a stride down the walkway that led to the public sidewalk. Ana stopped where the sidewalk met her walkway. The man jumped into a neon-green Dodge Charger and turned the ignition.

Seconds later, he was down the street and speeding away from Ana and Roxanne.

Ana returned to the house and walked in. She slammed the door behind her.

God Has a Sense of Humor

*T*HREE WORDS… *GET a life.* Yes, that was it. Something I had been told to acquire for the past 15 years.

The alarm clock sounded. I woke up on my stomach. Without looking, I reached over and turned the alarm off. I rolled over and stared at the ceiling. The popcorn design faded, and I imagined that I was peering into the afternoon sky. Alabaster clouds were everywhere. The sun shined brightly. Birds were flying in the distance. They were making their way towards me as I stared back at them from the ground. Their dark form came into view. One had fallen from its course. It tumbled to the ground towards me. As it fell, I brace myself for impact, covering my face…

"Mom, wake up!" Ricky shouted. My eight-year-old son jumped on the bed.

The fantasy was over. I came back to reality. I was staring at my son while lying in bed.

I got out of bed and headed to the bathroom. Ricky followed me, tugging at my nightshirt. I smacked his tiny hand away, but he laughed. He thought I was playing a game.

Standing in the bathroom, I looked at myself in the vanity mirror. White crud partially coated my eyelids. My eyes were bloodshot crimson; the right eye looked redder than the left. My face had aged. Although I was 42, I looked a lot older, and I didn't like it. Motherhood and life can age anyone.

Ricky played with my electric toothbrush. He grabbed the white handle and pushed the power button. The buzzing sound flooded the bathroom. He turned it off and grabbed my Colgate toothpaste. Squeezing the exact amount on the brush's tip, he smiled then handed the toothbrush handle over to me. As I brush, he ran to my closet and grabbed a pair of jeans and sneakers. I couldn't fit the jeans he had brought me. Eventually, I'd donate them to Goodwill, a friend, or relative.

Ricky looked at me and he smiled. He was a mature eight-year-old. For the past five years, he and I had grown accustomed to being a duo. After I had divorced his dad, Robert, I knew I had to make a few, important changes. Robert was a good man. He worked as a high school teacher at an inner city school, one of the toughest in Broward County.

Unfortunately, we couldn't make it work.

He preferred to hang out with his friends than spending time with his family. His alcoholism got the better of him, resulting in a hospital stay. We had some good times. But enough was enough. My baby boy and I needed to get out and fast.

I left Robert for a better life.

His mother hated me for it. She and I had a close relationship. That day I told her, she and I were sitting in her living room, watching her favorite show, *Golden Girls*. We would even joke about being roommates in the future when our kids were no longer our priority and our lovers dead and gone. She was a good friend to me. I confessed to her that I wasn't happy, and she told me to work harder at making it work. I listened and really, really tried. But the waiting gnawed at my spirit. Two years passed then came the separation and then the papers arrived.

Reluctantly, he signed them. Then it was over.

I was raised a catholic. I wanted to be a believer, but a believer of what? The kneeling and praying didn't always work.

I guess God had a sense of humor.

Forty minutes later, my boy and I were walking down the street to the bus stop. Ricky walked beside me with his navy blue EastPak on his back. He was humming some song I couldn't make out. Musical kid. I looked down at him. As he aged, he reminded me so much of Robert. The way he walked, talked, and ate. He was a younger, splitting image of his father.

And I hated it.

The bus arrived, and I gave Ricky a kiss before he had boarded the bus. He liked to sit on the right-hand side. Once he was on the bus, he took a seat at the window towards the middle of the bus. He waived at me. Another school day and another memory made. Years from now, I would cherish this moment.

The second half of the day was busy… work

Sitting in my office, I perused the area listings. Miramar had eight new listings and Pembroke Pines had twelve. Real estate was booming in those days. It was definitely a seller's market. Last year, I sold more than 20 properties within the first two quarters. International investors made the best clients. They brought international coins to American real estate, which equaled a major commission for *yours truly*. Competitor agents were bloodhounds. They could sniff out and pounce on a good deal quickly. A couple of listings were near my office. I grabbed my purse, keys, and phone, and then I was out the door.

The first listing was a large 1,700 square-foot, single-family home. The listing is a four-bedroom, two-bathroom house. It had been vacant for about a week. The owners relocated due to work, leaving a local relative to close the estate. The Silver Lakes was a fine community for families. I was confident that I could get the place sold and occupied within two months or fewer.

I arrived at the home.

The lockbox was located on west side of the house. I entered the code and released the latch. There was a silver, deadbolt key. I used the key to open the front door. Once inside, I was breath-taken.

The scent of wood filled the foyer. Dark wood was everywhere. The house was unfurnished. A beautiful walkway chandelier hung in the dining area. To my left was the entryway to the first main area, the kitchen. The owners had put a lot of money into the home. Pearl granite countertops with a gray and white backsplash provided a sophisticated charm. The Whirlpool appliances were all modern and energy efficient. Buyers would certainly love the finishes.

Then I head a sound at the front door. The door opened and immediately closed. Footsteps were approaching me from the hallway. I braced myself for the encounter.

"Hello?" I said.

"Hello," replied the voice. The voice sounded familiar.

Rita Montgomery walked in and placed her purse on the island countertop. We had known each other for years. At one point, we had worked at the same real estate firm. Eventually, she left to start her own practice, and it paid off. Rita was worth a good seven figures after overhead payout.

"Look at you, darling," she said.

We hugged. I faked cordiality.

"How long as it been? A year or two?" I asked.

"Long enough. So you're boss is after this one too?" she asked as she walked around the kitchen and surveyed the space. "Nice upgrades."

"Yes, and I intend to sell it," I assured her.

"Not if I don't get it first," she challenged.

We faced each other and smiled. I noticed a hint of red lipstick on her teeth. I laughed. She frowned.

"What's so funny?" She asked.

"Nothing," I lied. I tried to keep from laughing. "The listing states its valued at $610,000, but I think it's worth more."

"It is worth more. The owners were dear friends of mine. I used to visit. I saw its transformation," she said.

"That still doesn't give you the advantage," I added. But I knew it did. Any agent with an inside connection with the client was bound to win the sale. A slight pain entered my stomach. I felt defeated.

"Well, I will leave you to your work. If I leave before you, I'll lock up. Take care," Rita said.

She walked out of the kitchen.

Good grief. Some people could be annoying. Rita took the cake.

The backyard was a man cave's paradise. The previous owners had installed a custom-made fire pit with space for a barbeque. A wet bar with faucet was there too. The built-in seating was tasteful. The day was warm and humid. I walked a little further to the bar's edge. The lawn was manicured and fertilized. That would certainly add to the sale.

My ringtone chimed.

"May I speak to Ms. Brooks, please?" The woman asked.

"This is she," I responded.

"My name is Paula Sanchez. I called you yesterday about the house in Miramar," she said.

"Yes, thank you for returning my call. I'm here at the property now."

"I'm really interested in buying it. I'm actually in the area. I'm not sure if you're available to join me, but can I meet you at the house?" she asked.

"Of course, I look forward to meeting you. You have the address?" I asked.

"Yes. Thank you. I'll see you in 10 minutes."

Ninety minutes later, my new client and I are ending the tour of the home. I learned a lot about her. She and I had several things in common. She was a single mom, like me. She had a ten-year-son, and I had a charming eight-year-old. She was an accomplished professional, working as a medical doctor. And she was quite a looker, a woman who took good care of herself physically. As Rita walked out with her clients, she smiled at us both. We responded the same. A young man and his wife followed Rita out.

I promised Paula that I would follow up on her offer within the next day or so.

As she drove away, I couldn't help but notice a boy sitting at the bus stop across the way. He looked about Ricky's age, and he had a concerned look on his face. I was puzzled. What was a young boy doing at a county bus stop by himself?

I stood there, staring at the boy. He was toying with a cellphone in his lap. He pressed a few buttons and looked up. Finally, our eyes met. He smiled faintly, yet the concerned look on his face had returned. He was wearing a white t-shirt with the Dolphins logo on the front.

Something was wrong. A child his age should have been in school at that time of the day.

I walked over to the boy. I briefly examined his face. He had been crying. His eyes were pinkish and his hands were shaking a little. My motherly instincts kicked in. I took a seat next to him.

"What's your name?" I asked.

"Sam," he said.

"Where are you going?"

"I really don't know," he responded. He looked at me. Sad, pleading eyes spoke the truth. My heart melted. The boy was looked scared.

"What do you mean?" I continued. "Where are your parents? Do you have a brother or sister?"

"My mom told me to wait here until she got back," he said.

"She left you?" I asked. I was shocked.

I grew numb with pain. The thought of this happening to my own kid nearly killed me. I stared at Sam, who looked so confused and scared.

I had to do something.

Without thinking, we were back in my car and on our way to the police station. This child needed help. I phoned work. I spoke to the secretary and told her everything.

At the police station, I did what I could to make Todd feel comfortable.

"Do you like sports?" I asked.

"I love sports. I play football and basketball."

"I used to play basketball in high school. It's my favorite," I said.

"You played basketball?!" He asked in shock.

I smiled and said, "Yes, girls can do the same things boy can do."

"I know," he replied. He looked down at his phone.

"Don't be sad, Todd. Someone who love you will be here to get you soon. I'll stay here until they get here," I promised.

Todd smiled. He grabbed my arm. He wanted to be loved.

"I wish you were my mom," he confessed.

I looked at him. I did everything I could to keep from crying.

I stayed with Todd until a family member arrived to pick him up. When his grandmother arrived, she embraced him as if they hadn't seen each other in a long time.

Then the woman walked over to me and hugged me too. No words were exchanged. We did what mothers were expected to do.

Later, I picked up Ricky from aftercare. He jumped in the car; he was excited as usual to tell me about his day.

"I got first place on my science project, mom!" He yelled. He presented a blue ribbon.

"Awesome!" I exclaimed.

I held back the tears. The moment was very special. I also thought of Todd.

"You okay, mom?" Ricky asked. "Are you crying?"

"Yes, baby. I'm crying. Because I'm happy to see you, that's all," I said.

I drove home. Just when I thought I wasn't dissatisfied with what I didn't have, two boys reminded me to be grateful for what I did have all along.

Other Duties
As Assigned

I DON'T HAVE TO wear my gayness like a novelty t-shirt. I'm not in the closet. I don't plan to hop back in one either. But coming out is a never-ending process.

These thoughts ran through Jason's mind each time he started a new job and met new co-workers. A decade and four retail stores later, he found himself working at the Southland Mall in South Dade, a suburban community in Miami. After a referral and one interview, he landed the job as assistant store manager at H & M. The new role came with a bigger paycheck, something Jason needed. When he wasn't working, he attended the local community college, completing courses toward an associate's degree.

"Big plans for the little man," his mother would tease.

Everyone at his work knew he was out though at first it was hard to tell. On the surface, he looked like a typical, twenty-something jock with a "low-boy" hair cut and dark, Latino features. With hazel eyes, a goatee and pierced, diamond-stud earrings, Jason's *milkshake* brought the boys and the girls to the *yard*. Standing 5' 10" with a medium, slightly muscular build, he was a complete package. *Baby mama* or *boy toy* material, so to speak, easy on the eyes.

Jason's best friend, Nicole, was another store associate. They have known one another since middle school. Their science teacher would routinely sit students in alphabetical order: Jason Martinez and Nicole Mendez. For half a year, they didn't speak but by the end of the school year, they had forged a strong friendship. Years later, Jason dubbed Nicole his official *fag hag*. As derogatory as it sounded, the title was hers; she vowed to have his back no matter what.

One day while sitting in the break room, Nicole shared gossip, her favorite pastime.

"I heard your boss is DL (down low)," she said.

"And what's that got to do with me?" Jason asked.

"I'm just saying. I see the way he looks at you. It's weird. I think he likes you."

"Shuutt up!" Jason exclaimed. "He approves my payroll, we're not getting down like that, and I'm not about that. I need my job." He gave her an earnest look.

"Next time he's around, just watch. Your gaydar needs a tune-up, boy." They chuckle.

Two days later, Jason was scheduled to work the evening shift. Nick Richardson, his boss, also worked late at the store on select nights.

Jason, wearing ear buds, was in the backroom counting inventory. His work playlist is in full swing. Normani's "Motivation" bumped through the ear buds. Boxes of new arrivals, jeans and hoodies, awaited the sales floor. He enjoyed inventorying because he was off the floor and away from complaining customers and stressed-out associates.

Jason opened a box to examine its contents. The smell of new denim was hypnotizing. After the tenth pair of jeans, he took the stack and moved it toward the entrance. He repeated the process until nearly every box of jeans was empty and stacks of folded merchandise were prepped for the sales floor.

Jason surveyed the last box of jeans and boxes of hoodies to be opened. He calculated that they would take a couple of hours more to complete. He changed his music to David Guetta's Techno playlist. Usually reserved for the gym, Jason figured the song options would keep him moving at a pace and passing time more quickly. "Titanium", Jason's favorite song, played in his ears. He began to move his shoulders to the rhythm. He swayed his hips and grooved as he worked.

After unboxing and prepping the final stack of jeans, he placed it on a table with other stacks. As he walked, he moved to the music's beat, adding a few pelvic thrusts. Then he turned around to start on the first box of hoodies...

Jason jumped when he saw his boss.

He removed his ear buds and stuck them in his jeans' pocket.

"Don't stop on my account."

"I'm sorry, Nick. I didn't know you were there."

"It's okay," Nick said while staring at Jason.

"Uh, do you need something?" Jason asked.

"Yes," he replied. "Where is last night's closeout report? I want to compare it to today's figures."

"It's on the desk back in the office."

"Thanks," Nick said.

Jason turned around to return to his work. He could feel Nick watching him from behind. Eventually, Nick left.

Three days later, Jason received an email from Nick stating that he'd return to the store during Jason's shift to discuss sales projections. Nick asked if Jason wouldn't mind remaining for an extra hour to go over numbers.

When Jason arrived to work hours later, he found Nick sitting in the office, peering over sales reports. Nick greeted him with a smile.

"Take a seat, Jason," he said.

Jason sits across from him.

"Is something wrong?"

"No. But… I must say I'm impressed with your work."

"Thank you, Nick. That means a lot. I just want to do a good job."

"Believe me, you are…" Nicks said, smiling.

Nick's tone makes Jason uncomfortable.

Jason noticed a charcoal-colored, wedding band. Nick kept smiling and moved his hand away, out of view.

"I locked up. Mike and Cynthia are still on the floor closing sales," Jason said, keeping the conversation focused on work.

Nick turned to his computer screen.

"I can't seem to figure out one figure though. Sit here and look at this Excel chart," Nick got up and walked away from the desk. Jason hesitated, then walked around the desk to sit in Nick's chair.

"What do you want me to see?"

"Look at that column," Nick said, pointing to a yellow-highlighted column with green and red figures. "I'm not sure why February 22nd is inaccurate."

Nick towered over Jason. Jason caught a whiff of Nick's cologne. Nick began to press into the right side of Jason's back.

"Look at that number…" Nick continued, pressing further.

Jason felt something else pressing against him. Nick, erect, grinded into Jason's back.

Repulsed, Jason pushed him away and leaped out of the chair.

"I know you want it," Nick said. He grabbed Jason's arm and pulled Jason's hand to his crotch. "Come on, you faggots like straight men."

Disgusted, Jason got up and left.

Nick's advances continued. Sexual remarks in the break room and occasional gropes after closing become routine. Jason started calling out sick each time Nick was scheduled to work with him.

Nicole's intuition got the better of her one afternoon. She questioned Jason.

"He makes me sick, Nicole. I can't stand him."

"Come on. He's just teasing you. He can't be serious. Ok?" She touched Jason's hand in assurance. He retreated.

Being a gay man doesn't give him the right to treat me like a piece of meat, he thought.

One month later, Jason was transferred to another store, wearing his gayness like a wedding gown. On the outside he looked fine, but on the inside, he felt bruised and violated.

His new boss, Myra, introduced herself.

"You deserve a medal," she said boldly. "You worked for my ex-husband, Nick Richardson. Looking forward to working with you."

Jason smiled. They had something in common.

A Woman's Revenge

*M*ANY PEOPLE HAVE *done things that they later live to regret.* "I'm sorry" *won't fix every mistake. People make choices... to stay the course and weather the storm or run for cover, hoping someone will forget your transgressions...*

Anita chose the former.

She chose to remain with him even when her heart said otherwise.

While preparing dinner, Anita spoke to her son, Michael. Michael sat at the dining table working on his Algebra homework. As he worked, Anita watched him. She smiled. Then she continued preparing spaghetti and meatballs. The water boiled wildly and ready to cook pasta. Anita broke open the box, poured a handful of pasta into her hand, and broke up the long strands into smaller, consumable strands. She repeated this ritual until the box was empty.

"I'm making your favorite, baby," she reminded her son.

"Thanks, ma," he responded. "Did you add mushrooms? I hate those."

"Hate is such a harsh word, baby," she said.

"Okay, I *dislike* mushrooms," he responded sarcastically. They chuckled.

"But dad likes mushrooms, remember?" he recalled.

"I know, but this is your night," Anita replied.

"Yeah, not like *Algebra...*" he said while pointing to the open textbook.

In the distance, Anita and Michael heard the front door open and close. Max, their Golden Retriever, began barking enthusiastically.

Josue arrived home.

He was a big man. His entire frame absorbed nearly all the space in the kitchen's doorway. His clothing *wore him*. Sporting a beer belly and large, tree trunk legs, Josue had ballooned an extra 80 pounds after fourteen years of marriage, work, and stress.

Josue greeted Michael with a head rub. They had a special bond, considering Michael was his step son and the only father the boy had known. Anita glanced in Josue's direction, faintly smiling at her husband.

The house waivered with the smells of good cooking. The heat from the boiling water teased Anita's face. Behind her sat Josue and Michael, exchanging dialogue about their days. Michael talked about his crush who sat behind him in fourth period math. He wanted to ask her out on a date. Josue listened intently as his step son chatted away. Anita eavesdropped though pretending to be immersed in her cooking.

"I think she knows I like her," Michael continued.

"Then ask her out. It's that simple. Do you think she likes you?" Josue asked.

"I'm not sure. But I feel crazy good when I'm around her. I won't even turn around when she talks. I guess I'm a shy," Michael confessed.

"Take it from me. I know women..." Josue advised.

Anita frowned in disapproval.

"What should I do?" Michael asked.

"Let her know where you stand or she'll just run away," Josue said.

"That's not true," Anita intervened. "Be a gentleman and be courteous. That's how *I* raised you."

Josue remained silent. Michael looked at his mother who stared sternly at Josue.

"I think this is my cue to leave," Michael said as he gathered up his study materials to exit the kitchen. He left soon after.

Anita and Josue sat across from one another. For a while, a wall had been drawn between the two. And each knew the reasons why. While the food simmered, they both new it was time to confirm or release whatever demons were destroying their relationship. Josue's eyes met hers. The silence dominated.

"What are we doing, Josue?" Anita asked.

"You tell me…" He looked at his wife with sad, pleading eyes.

"It's hard to erase the stains, the pain. You know that," she responded while keeping her eyes gazing on him.

"I didn't mean to do it, but it happened. You said you forgave me."

"But the forgetting is impossible," she said as she tapped her index finger on the table. "You hurt me… bad."

"Damn it, woman! I told you I'm sorry. What more do you want from me?" he exclaimed while slamming his right hand down on the table.

"I want you to feel just an ounce of the pain you caused me. That's my only request." A wide grin crossed her face.

Josue stomped out of the room.

Hours later, Anita was in her master bathroom, blow drying her long, permed hair. The day was long and she wanted to clear her mind. Washing her hair always relaxed her. She had beautiful hair with hints of gray on the edges.

I think I need a touch-up, she thought.

As she worked her hair, she looked at herself in the mirror. Eventually, her eyes met her own in the mirror's reflection. She didn't recognize the woman staring back at her anymore. Years had set in. Her beauty still flourished, but somewhere deep down inside resided a hate that love and forgiveness could not mend. The more Anita stared, the angrier she grew.

Why do women stay in relationships they know are not right for them? No woman can change any man.

She was beyond that stage. More negative thoughts and rhetorical questions wrestled in her mind. She needed answers and closure.

Josue cheated on her... this was a fact. Or rather he lied.

Anita could recall the day she discovered his first attempt at infidelity. Anita had just arrived home from work when Josue called her to announce that his aunt Gloria had just arrived from Cuba. The family planned to gather later that evening at his mother's house over in Hialeah. Wine bottles, Latin food and Cuban music were part of the menu.

"I'll be there by 7," Anita promised.

Not even thirty minutes later, she received another call.

"Babe, have you left the house yet?" Josue inquired.

"I'm walking out the door. Why?"

"Well, I kinda got into a little trouble," he responded.

"What *kind* of trouble?"

"I... I was arrested..."

Anita dropped the cellphone.

"Babe... babe..." Josue begged from the phone on the floor.

His voice faded in the distance. Later she learned the reason... Josue was arrested for soliciting an undercover female cop for prostitution.

He shouldn't have done it, but he did. And *that* mad her mad as hell.

Anita placed the blow dryer back on its charging station and turned off the bathroom light. She was immersed in impenetrable darkness... for a moment. Eventually, her eyes adjusted; she surveyed her surroundings. She could make out a faint, white, and massive image on the bed. Snoring flooded the room. Josue was asleep. His nocturnal apparatus, his sleeping machine, was on and humming a faint, annoying sound. His doctor prescribed the machine to help him breath as he slept. The machine helped him surely, but it made it even harder for Anita to rest.

Anita slowly walked into the bedroom, calculating each step like a cat stalking its prey. One, two, three, then a right turn… five more and then she reached her hand out to grasp for something. *A cold, flat wall, or door,* she thought. Running her right hand downward, she searched for something else. She rubbed along the ridges and found… the closet's doorknob.

Squeakkkkkk!

The closet door's track was rusty and noisy, but the sleeping machine drowned the squeaking. Kneeling in the darkness, she rummaged in the abyss for something familiar. She ran her hands across what felt like a shoelace. Reaching further, she noticed more… a shirt or teddy bear, or maybe a feathered boa. Then she felt something squirmy and plastic. Her index finger ran across its ridges. Whatever it was, it was long, odd, and had a groove in its bottom. She pushed deeply into the groove.

A buzzing, vibrating object began to compete with the sleeping machine… a dildo.

With both hands, Anita grabbed the toy and immediately switched it off. She tossed it back into the bottomless pit in the closet.

Resuming her search, she continued on for what seemed like ten minutes or so. Growing hopeless, she pushed her way to the farthest reaches of the floor and found nothing.

As Anita stood, her hand grazed another object.

"That's it," she thought.

She found what she was looking for. She scooped it up in one hand and turned toward the bed.

Slowly, she approached the sleeping Yeti, her husband. The machine hummed even more loudly to the point of sheer aggravation.

In the darkness, she imagined her husband peacefully sleeping. His large belly and chest rose and fell, sucking up or blowing out oxygen. Josue was in a deep sleep.

Humans are fascinating, strong creatures. But there are two times in the day when we are most vulnerable… one is when we're in the shower, and the other is when we're in the bed. When we're in the shower, we're one with nature, soaking, scrubbing, and washing away the day's grime. When we sleep, we're one with our own conscious. If anything were to happen while engaging in the two activities, well, the outcome is unknown. Crazy thoughts ran through Anita's mind.

Then she cracked a devious smile.

Swiftly, she pulled the sheets back off of her husband. She yanked the machine's chords and mask off too. In the shadows, she raised her right hand high above her head, and in it, she held the object salvaged from the closet floor...

Her wide, summer sandal, the *chancleta.*

She started beating Josue's black, fat ass.

She hit his stomach and his large left tit. Sparing no mercy, she made her way to his tree trunk thighs.

Josue was immediately awakened.

"What the hell is your problem?!" he exclaimed, trying to defend himself from his estranged wife.

Anita continued to whip him with that shoe. Whatever resided in her had finally manifested into physical reality, and she felt good doing hurting him.

"I'm calling the police!" he screamed.

Anita stopped assaulting him. Her soul was dark and cold.

"And if you do, you'll be a dead man," she retorted.

After a minute, she dropped the chancleta. It landed on the floor. She left the room. She emasculated Josue.

Then suddenly, Anita felt a surge of vindication. She had achieved what she should have done a long time ago. Her actions could have sent her to jail, but she didn't care. He shouldn't have done what he had done.

She walked down the hallway. The family room's lights were still on and gleaming in the distance like a light at the end of a tunnel. Darkness was the midwife, helping her birth a new being, someone she no longer wanted to hide. Once in the family room, she sat on the crimson loveseat.

Josue waddled into the room, nursing his right forearm, wearing only boxers. Anita could see the bruises on his legs and chest.

The sight of him bothered her.

"I'm going to Walmart. Do you need anything?" She offered with a smile. But speechless, Josue just stared at her.

After getting ready, she was in her ca heading to the store. She was done with caring for his feelings or what others would say about her in the aftermath.

He shouldn't have done what he had done. There's nothing worse than a woman scorn. There's nothing worse than a woman's revenge. At last, justice for the black widow.

Waiting for an Appointment

*I*T WAS NOT until the latter years of my life when I realized that the idea of waiting was lost forever. For centuries humankind had forced itself to wait on *something*... an opportunity, a paycheck, a baby's delivery. Waiting and anticipation are strange cousins. Their relationship is dysfunctional, but somehow, they manage to get along... inside of me.

This office looked so unfamiliar. Everywhere I looked, I saw alabaster white. The white chairs were strategically aligned to form a letter of some sort. Most of them were empty, except for one that was occupied by an elderly man with a certain smile. He looked vaguely familiar. The remainder of the space looked typical. A flat-screen television played a family-friendly show that didn't interest me. The sign-in clipboard rested on a pearl-white counter top. A service bell was placed nearby the clipboard to signal the arrival of a new patient. There was no clock in the waiting room.

I looked down at my watch, and strangely, it too had stopped working. The last time it worked was 3:00... a.m. or p.m.? I couldn't remember.

And for some reason, I couldn't find my phone. Usually, I'd watch a YouTube video or surf the internet. And I never left home without my phone.

The door opened and a middle-aged woman entered pushing a baby's stroller. She was dressed in a beautiful Sunday dress decked in pure, solid white. Her skin was olive and her eyes slanted. Either she was Latin or biracial, with a hint of Asian. Whatever she was, she was stunningly beautiful. She approached the counter and rang the bell. The sound of the bell resonated throughout the waiting room.

I was in a waiting room.

The service window opened and an elderly woman greeted the woman. No words were exchanged, only smiles. Their actions indicated that the two may have known each other. The elderly woman glanced over at the stroller and smiled again. Strange. Usually women are very chatty when it comes to children and motherhood. But no conversation of that sort was happening.

The service window closed and the middle-aged woman pushed her stroller to a nearby seat... across from me.

Everything about her was special. In fact, her actions were so direct, so specific, that it felt like I was watching her move in slow motion. After propping her purse on the seat next to her, she pulled the stroller toward her. Slight coos could be heard. The baby was awake but very well behaved. The mother left the baby in the strolling. After all, it wasn't crying.

The woman looked at me.

She was so beautiful. Her lips were a slight carnation pink. But her eyes. They were dark and inviting. Something about her made me want to get to know her more. Then she smiled again. That smile could light up a thousand dark nights or melt an iceberg in...

Wait a minute... that smile was too familiar.

I froze.

The woman was someone I'd known from long ago. Peggy Repelton was her name. She was my mother's best friend. I didn't know what to do. Usually, I'm a pretty social person. But Peggy's presence struck a cord in me.

Peggy had been dead for nearly ten years.

"Brandon, look at you!" She exclaimed. Her beauty was even more captivating when she spoke.

"How… where… where did you…" I stammered.

"Come from?" she continued. "Yeah, I get that a lot. You look good, B. So good to see you. How's your mom?"

"Great…" was all I could say, for I was still mesmerized at speaking to a dead woman.

"Well, it must be your first time here. Don't worry, you'll be fine," she assured me.

"Honestly, I don't even know why I'm here."

"That's understandable. It'll make sense once you go in to see the doctor," she said.

The smell of baby powder filled the air. Then I remembered the baby in the stroller. I glanced at the stroller and Peggy caught my eye. She smiled again.

"This is my daughter," Peggy introduced. She turned the stroller toward me to allow me to peer inside. I got up and walked over to examine the baby…

"There's nothing here, Peggy! What are you doing?" I shouted and retreated back to my seat. "This isn't funny."

The door opened and another patient entered. He wore a seersucker, ivory suite with baby-blue pinstripes. After signing the clipboard, he sat two seats to the right of Peggy, with the stroller between Peggy and him. His demeanor was not that welcoming… nor was his face. I recognized that face from anywhere.

"Mr. Decentes," I spoke. The man looked in my direction. With a puzzled look, he just stared at me.

"What are you doing here?" He asked.

"What are *you* doing here?" I retorted.

Mr. Decentes and I were not on the best of terms. A few months ago he decided to decline my vacation leave last minute. For months I had been planning an escape to the Virgin Islands with my wife, Evelyn. The critter decided it was best that I remain in town to manage the office while he took a vacation of his own. *That* was the problem. His plans always mattered over everyone else's.

Peggy and Decentes looked at each other but did not say a word. They both stared at me. Peggy was a kind woman. She always treated me with respect and allowed me to jump the fence when my football would go over the fence into her yard. Her son, Chris, was a year younger than I. After high school, he and I parted ways due to college and life… life.

Life was the one thing that stayed with us until the very end. It shaped us and defined us in every capacity. It also decided to check out on us when it had had enough. I grew confused. Life had left Peggy a long time ago. But I had just seen Decentes a week ago.

"Don't even ask, Brandon. It will all make sense," he spoke out of nowhere. His voice usually would irritate me. But this time, something was different. There was a hint of sincerity in it, something I had not heard for a very long time from him. In fact, it had been so long ago that it made me question if the man were even human.

"I don't understand," I said.

He looked away and stared at the white wall across from him, waiting for his appointment.

My stomach felt unsettled. To steady my nerves, I tried to occupy myself with something to do, to keep from focusing on the two patients who I strangely knew so well. But there were no magazines or other reading material available in the waiting room, except for the flat-screen TV playing some unknown Hallmark flick.

A middle-aged man had given a rose to the woman in the scene. They embraced and the credits began to roll. The woman looked so familiar too. After the credits, the couple remained on the screen. They kissed and then looked out at the audience.

For a moment, I thought they were looking directly at me. The screen went blank for a moment, only to loop yet another, exciting Hallmark feature.

Peggy began to rock the stroller back and forth to comfort the invisible baby. Her movement silenced it. Pleased, Peggy opened her purse and pulled out a book to read. The book's cover flashed my way.

Life after the Suffering... classic.

The door opened again. This time a man about my age entered the room. He wore a white tank top, cargo pants and beach sandals. I immediately recognized him.

"Mark?!" I shouted. I got up to hug him.

"Man, it's good to see you finally made it," he replied.

"Can you explain what's going on here? I'm so confused."

"B, it will make sense after you see the doctor," he assured.

He took a seat next to me. He didn't even bother to sign in.

"Bruh, are you here *for* me?" I inquired. I looked directly at his face.

Mark's face was clear and bright. His zits were gone; they were replaced with clean lines and tight, youthful skin. His parents were of Native American-descent. He reminded me of a modernized, young Indian warrior who had returned home after a long battle. Mark possessed the kind of look that made girls smile and mothers wish their daughters could marry him. He glanced over at Peggy and then at Decentes. They smiled back.

I glanced up at the flat-screen TV. The new Hallmark special had begun. A young black boy carried a basket as he walked toward a crop. He kneeled to pick pole beans. A black woman, assumedly his mother, called to him. He dropped the basket and scurried to her side. Hugging her he looked out at the camera to the audience. That boy was so cute. His innocence knew nothing of the world that awaited him. That boy... wait... couldn't be...

No, it couldn't be.

Suddenly, I sat up, causing Mark to stir a bit, but he didn't speak.

I was the boy on the screen.

And then the moment returned. I had remembered the day my mother and I volunteered in Homestead, Florida, to pick beans for the migrant families that would consume them. When I had first volunteered, I thought it was the worst thing in the world. Working under the sweltering Florida sun to pick food that I would never eat. My eight-year-old mind pondered, *Why can't those families pick their own damn beans? How come we have to do this every Saturday morning when it didn't rain? And how come I never get the chance to meet the migrant families?* At least they should say *thank you* for the work we did.

I was ignorant back then in the night. I knew nothing of the world.

There were questions that I wanted answers to. *Like, what exactly lives in the Mariana Trench? Why are bees suddenly dying? Or how did Donald Trump get elected?* If science was to remain as silent or confused as I was, then surely it would not have any answer or explanation to the moment I was having. I steadied my nerves and tried with all my power to remain calm. But I was irritated with confusing and a hint of rage. The smell of baby powder entered the air. Peggy rocked the stroller once more to soothe the invisible baby.

"You don't have to apologize," Mark said. He stared at the wall in front of him.

"Look, I know but I didn't mean for it to end that way," I added.

"It was meant to be. That's how life is," he said.

"But life doesn't always have to be that way. It still matters to me, man."

"But it won't matter for long. Everything is fine. Here we are again as friends," he replied, patting me on my left leg while keeping his eyes on the wall.

"Thank you."

The memories of a broken friendship began to haunt me. We had a good thing going. But certain situations got the better of us. That situation drove a wedge between us, and then it Mark flashed a passport in my face.

He booked that trip and was never heard from again. Not until five years later when he was found dead in the lake behind his mother's house. *Suicide*, they said. *Abandonment?* That was more appropriate.

The waiting room's door opened one more time. A dark-haired lady, about sixty, entered the room. She walked to the counter to announce her arrival, ringing the bell and signing in. She glanced at each of us and spoke only with a smile. Her attire looked as if it were from another era. Her snow-white dress draped all the way to the floor. The train was a bit too long. She was overdressed for her doctor's appointment and even more so, out of era.

"Hello, Ms. Crawford," Mark greeted. Ms. Crawford responded with a smile.

Then she walked pass us. The began to smell like Channel No. 5. The woman took a seat at the far end of the room, away from everyone else. I recognized her as well.

She was the late Joan Crawford, bitch-actress extraordinaire.

Thoughts entered my mind once again. Decentes knew I always hated him. Peggy was my mother's best friend and my first crush. Mark was my ride-or-die boy. And Joan Crawford, well, she was my outlet every time I got in the mood to be nostalgic and reminded that I was as fucked up as the rest of the world. Of all the places to be, I never thought I'd be in a waiting room with a motley crew like this.

The inner office door leading to the doctor suddenly opened. Out walked a male attendant, wearing platinum scrubs and holding a clipboard.

"Mr. Brandon Johnson..." he announced.

Confused, I walked over to him. I passed each of the waiting room's visitors. Each looked at me. Suddenly, I heard a thought...

"You'll be okay after you see him."

It was Mark.

I looked at him and he returned a smile. In life this man never smiled as much as he did then. Whoever this doctor was, I hoped he could fix me the way he had fixed Mark.

A year later I was back in the waiting room for my annual check-up. So much had changed since the first day I arrived to meet the doctor. But after my session, all became clear. The diagnosis was simple and the medication, effective. I had made such progress. I ended up moving away, far away, and changing my employment to retirement.

My family was so sad that I left. From a distance, I watched my mother weep and raise her hands to the world. Her rage could shake the universe. But it was the required order of things. I needed to go. Soon, she and I would reunite in an unfamiliar place and time.

Mark and I would see each other every day. We sometimes play ball together or talk on the phone until late at night. In a new place it was important to make new friends even with familiar, old faces.

Decentes and I had long since buried our differences. Even he had become a confidant of sorts. I only wish we had developed this relationship long ago. Things would have been different.

Peggy and I have dinner on occasion. She is so busy with other matters. Even I have opted to babysit the invisible baby for her. Babysitting was easy too. It didn't need to be changed or fed. But it did get loud occasionally. Peggy was the only one capable of nurturing it.

And I finally learned the baby's name: *Memory*. How fitting.

The waiting room was a special place. New patients had arrived. I was assigned to meet one of them… Susan. Yes, Susan. We were acquainted a long time ago. *I don't think she is expecting me.* Mark trained me well. I knew what to do.

With a puzzled look, Susan stared at me when I arrived. I smiled. No words or sounds. Just smiles. She grinned. But confusion won her over; I could see it in her face. I knew that feeling once.

She'll be okay after she sees the doctor, I thought.

When the Time Comes

"*HI, BRENTON. This is Yolanda, John Yarborough's wife. I have something very important to tell you. Can you please call me as soon as possible? Thanks.*"

Brenton closed the instant messenger app after reading the message from his stepmother. It had been years since he had heard from his father's side of the family.

He dialed the number. Someone picked up the line.

"Yolanda, this is Brenton," he spoke.

"Hi, Brenton. It's Yolanda. I hope you're doing okay. I have something to tell you."

"Okay, what's going on?" He asked.

"Your father… he passed away last night in his sleep."

Brenton felt a sharp pain in his stomach. Everything started to move in slow motion. He checked the time on his iPhone… 11:39 a.m. His body became numb. He didn't know what to feel or who to call first. Over the years, he witnessed the passing of dear friends and colleagues' parents. He was there to provide solace and support for all of them. Now this.

He was inducted into a new class of people: children who'd lost a parent.

Yolanda had discovered his father early that morning around 5:30 a.m. They were early birds. Yolanda had gotten up, gone to the bathroom and washed her face. John stayed in bed and waited his turn in the bathroom. She took a shower, put on clothes, and drank coffee while the 6 o'clock news played in the background. This morning ritual went on for nearly 27 years.

She walked to John's side of the bed to kiss him goodbye. She touched his hand... no response. She pushed him a little harder and still there was no reply. Then she felt his forehead. He was slightly warm. John's eyes were partially open; he didn't blink. Placing her right index finger under his nose, she checked to see if he was breathing.

John was dead.

Brenton called his mother to tell her the news. In 1974, she and John had separated less than a year after Brenton had been born. The couple was so young and in love. Her parents forbade it, but love prevailed. In time a child was born. And then things changed. The couple began to fight. Their loved had hardened like a burnt pie's crust. And no one enjoyed burn pie. Finally, the relationship ended.

Brenton's mother, Brenda, wanted to marry John and was determined to do so. They wanted to elope, but Brenda's parents found out about it and stepped in. Brenda became so mad at her parents that she hopped in her Toyota and drove. She drove and drove and drove, heading west. Eventually, she arrived in Alabama then Louisiana. With $300 in her purse and anger as her tour guide, she fled South Florida to go only God knew where. To save on gas, she traveled with the windows down, embracing the natural air. The air in Alabama was so different than South Florida. It smelled of fresh-cut grass and cow manure. The landscape was so surreal. Suburban picket fences were replaced with green pastures and forests. There were very few streetlights. The roads were less congested. At one point, she was the only driver on a long, winding road toward infinity.

Brenda's grandparents raised Brenton the only way they knew how. Still raising seven of their own, they never fathomed they'd be grandparents at such a young age. The baby did not make himself. This life had a purpose. Brenton would receive the best they could offer him. As the years passed, Brenton grew taller and wiser. He was adept to music and the arts. A talkative eight-year-old, he would ask all kinds of questions about nature.

"Mama, why are all those birds on that line?" he asked, pointing to the extended line of black crows perched high on the electrical line.

They squawked loudly. Some of the birds would leave the line, flying high in the sky, only to return back to another space on the line and making more squawks in nature's symphony.

"From up north, baby," Mama said.

"Why? It's too hot here!" He exclaimed.

"They come here to keep warm. Like you are with us. We keep you warm."

She hugged Brenton tightly. Later she introduced a set of science encyclopedias to him that she kept out of reach on a Florida Pine bookshelf. The volumes were recent and colorful, containing all of the answers young Brenton had about science. For hours, he would spend peering over each book, examining pictures of great white sharks and coral reefs. Jacques Cousteau's picture appeared in every book, chronicling his explorations with memorable quotes. Brenton was an avid reader, yet he still could not make out all of the words in every passage. However, one passage intrigued him.

"Mama, can you read this? I don't know all the words."

Brenton pointed to a line on page 42.

"Okay, let me see…" Mama said, examining the line. "It says, *the sea, once it casts its spell, holds one in its net of wonder forever.*"

"Wow…" Brenton said as he stared at the vast sea on the page.

No land was visible for miles. Cousteau sailed gallantly to places only discovered in books or films.

"I want to be like him," Brenton said while pointing at a voyaging Cousteau.

"Be you, baby. Be who you want to be."

But the Johnson family had its share of secrets.

On their way to the bowling alley to play in a league, Pop and Brenton rode on in Pop's 1984 Cadillac Sedan. Twelve-year-old Brenton stared out of the passenger window. Pop lowered the car stereo's volume.

"I need to tell you something, Brenton," he said.

"What, Pop?" Brenton looked over at his grandfather.

Pop paused and then he said, "The lady at the house is not your mama."

Brenton was speechless and confused.

Suddenly, everything made sense. Brenton's cousin, Cassey, was his "cousin." *If I were her cousin, shouldn't I be her uncle instead?* The thought ran through his mind over and over. He couldn't believe he was adopted. He had to ask the question.

"Then who's my mama?"

There was a brief pause.

"Your sister, Brenda."

Those words, *your sister*, struck Brenton like a bat. Everything began to make sense. Brenton was told that he was the eighth child of the Johnson clan. His brothers, Darnell and William, were just ten and twelve years his senior respectively. Brenda was the eldest child followed by her sisters and then Uncle James, Jr., the first boy born in the family. The grandparents raised Brenton and Cassey. They were more like siblings than cousins.

That news challenged Brenton; he developed issues with trust. He was betrayed his entire life, and it made him mad. He loved his family dearly. His life was turned upside down.

Despite the deception, Brenton's childhood was fine. His fascination for science transformed into a fascination for language, the English language. For hours he would write the scripts to soap operas adapted from Mama's favorites, *Young and the Restless* and *All My Children*. He possessed the power of the pen, creating a world where the greatest dramas were about losing a dog or getting a new bike for Christmas. Each script was written in spiral-bound, unshared notebooks. Whenever something dramatic happened in the family, he would write it into a script.

He wrote about everything, except his own deception.

Years passed. Brenton attended college and started working as a high school teacher. At age 23, he was in grad school, making a decent living and reaching a new milestone—he was in the market to buy his first home, a condo. It was a buyer's market. He searched for a place close to work to save on gas and to avoid a lengthy commute. Everything was going well for him...

Until it was time to meet his biological father... for the first time.

The initial meeting was emotionally exhausting. They met at Brenton's workplace, a high school, in Coconut Grove. On the first Saturday of each month, Brenton supervised the school's service learning projects. By Noon, he was done with his work. By 12:45 p.m., all of the students were gone. Brenton remained in his office, reviewing paperwork and filing documents.

There was a knock at the door.

"Come in," Brenton invited. John entered the office.

Brenton saw pictures of his parents just before they completed high school. They were so young. Jason wore a black suit with a crimson tie and a black fedora. He was dressed like a mobster. Brenda wore a spaghetti-strapped, black dress with crimson polka dots. John stood behind her, hugging her lovingly. They looked happy.

Brenton studied his father. He realized how much he looked like him. Brenton had a solid, youthful build, and John was a fit man in his 40s.

John hugged his son. The moment was 23 years in the making.

"I'm so glad to see you," John said.

"Have a seat, John," Brenton said.

John sat next to him.

"You look great, son," Jason continued.

"So do you," Brenton replied.

Their eyes met. Brenton was filled with emotions.

"You probably wonder where I've been," Jason said.

"Actually, I don't," Brenton confessed. "My family showed me a picture of you with my mom. But they never spoke negatively of you."

"Really?" Jason asked in disbelief.

"It's like you didn't exist," Brenton confirmed.

They talked for another hour. Brenton learned about his father's parents. Both were still alive and anxious to meet Brenton. John admitted how Brenton's grandfather despised him for impregnating his daughter. Brenton listened as his father recounted a time when the grandfather pulled out a gun and threatened to take John's life. John was to stay away. Brenton had heard the story before from his mother's family. But all that was in the past.

Brenton decided to come out to John. John accepted him. John shared pictures of his wife and daughters, who were all eager to meet Brenton.

John promised him many, incredible things.

But the years went by and no one made calls. Brenton was too busy working and building an independent life. He called his father during New Year's Eve and promised to get together soon.

However, they never met up. It was so strange. Something kept Brenton away. His heart just wasn't in it.

When Yolanda called, Brenton thought it was an opportunity to reconnect with his father. He never fathomed that it would be under death's pretense.

John's viewing was scheduled a week later.

Brenton arrived to the funeral home to pay his final respects. It was a hot, pretty day. As Brenton entered the parlor, his half sister, Tanya, ran over to him and hugged him tightly. Together, they walked to the far end of the room.

They approached the casket.

John was dressed in an alabaster suit with red accents. Family members greeted Brenton, but he didn't know them; he didn't even know their names.

"You look so much like your father," an older woman said. She touched Brenton's left cheek.

They circled Brenton like he was a campfire, touching and hugging him.

But Brenton felt uneasy.

He felt no emotional tie to his father. And *that* bothered him. He had so many conflicting emotions. Above all, he felt bad for not *feeling bad*.

Death paid the final price.

CPSIA information can be obtained
at www.ICGtesting.com
Printed in the USA
BVHW031415311019
562603BV00004B/15/P